many
things
have
happened
since
he died

many
things
have
happened
since
he died

and here
are the
highlights...

elizabeth
dewberry
vaughn

DOUBLEDAY

New York

London

Toronto

Sydney

Auckland

PUBLISHED BY DOUBLEDAY
a division of
Bantam Doubleday Dell Publishing Group, Inc.
666 Fifth Avenue, New York, New York 10103

DOUBLEDAY and the portrayal of an anchor
with a dolphin are trademarks of Doubleday,
a division of Bantam Doubleday Dell Publishing
Group, Inc.

All of the characters in this book are fictitious,
and any resemblance to actual persons, living or
dead, is purely coincidental.

Library of Congress Cataloging-in-Publication Data
Vaughn, Elizabeth Dewberry.
Many things have happened since he died and here are the
highlights / by Elizabeth Dewberry Vaughn.—1st ed.
p.   cm.
I. Title.
PS3572.A936M3   1990
813'.54—dc20   89-11708
CIP

ISBN 0-385-26500-X

Copyright © 1990 by Elizabeth Dewberry Vaughn

All Rights Reserved
Printed in the United States of America
April, 1990
FIRST EDITION

BVG

This
book
is
for
Rob

The author
would like to thank
Elaine Markson
Lucy Herring
Nan A. Talese
Robert Detweiler
Clark Blaise
J. W. Dewberry
Jim Dewberry, Jr.
Sallie Dewberry
Robert Vaughn

chapter 1

My father has been dead 101 days.

I bet he is rotten. Amelia is rotten.

I got the duck he hung over the fireplace and we hung it over the sofa. He wiped off the blood and covered the bullet hole and fixed it so it looks like it never died. His father had a snake all coiled up like it was going to strike only it wouldn't obviously. But it makes you wonder can you ever be absolutely sure of anything. We kept the snake in the basement.

Mr. Brooks has a fox like that in his office. It bares its teeth at you when you go in there. Sometimes I go in there but I never look at that fox and if I do I never make eye contact. It stays inside a glass box on a table beside his sofa and you can see its reflection in the glass on the picture of his wife and two daughters that sits next to it. They are not very pretty. When I answer the phone they never ask how are you. If you are a lawyer it is easy to end up with brats for a family.

I am very nice to them, but not because I have to be. Because I am using them. They will do many good things for me. Like when I go to law school. Like now when I am using their dictaphone. Because making these tapes gives me a certain kind of power. Authority. I will never say to my secretary I need this done ASAP. I want a male secretary.

I used to want to be a taxidermist but now I don't. Could they do that to humans. It's probably against the law but I think they could. I wish they had before they buried him and then I wouldn't have to think about him rotting.

No I don't. When they do that they take out all your guts my father showed me one time and you should be buried with all your guts. Unless you were in some horrible accident and they fell out and nobody could help it. But you shouldn't take somebody else's guts out on purpose just to make yourself feel better. This is what I do. Satan tempts me with weak and selfish thoughts but I talk myself out of them and prove how strong I am. I believe God rewards the little things he who is faithful in little. I may have added a diamond to my crown just now by overcoming that selfish thought.

Many things have happened since he died. Here are the highlights:

Day 1	Death
Day 3	Funeral
Day 18	Engagement
Day 56	End of summer school
Day 73	Wedding
Day 74	Twentieth birthday
Day 76	Start job
Day 82	Malone starts dental school

I wonder if the coffin was airtight or if worms could get in. Two days after the funeral it rained hard for four hours straight and I tried not to think about it.

My father went to Florida and waded out into the ocean and died. They had to carry his body from the water over the crowded hotel beach and people thought he had drowned. Most of the people who had been horrified no delighted both to see a drowning victim and a possible suicide on their vacation never found out that it had been an ordinary heart attack.

Your father is dead your father is dead. Your father is in heaven. Our Father who art in heaven. Our father who is dead.

There is too much I cannot tell my father.

I never told him that I did not die when they wanted me to. I went under the water and held my breath and lay very still until they pulled me up. I wanted a true relationship with my father, but I could not die for it. I never told him about Malone.

5

Malone said that since our souls have been knitted together in love we are married in God's sight so wives submit yourselves to your husbands.

The Lord hates fornicators. I am not one I hate them too. I don't believe in it before marriage I really don't I don't know what happened. I had never before I was saving myself.

We are really married now which makes it not as bad. Bad I still don't condone it just not as bad.

I always wash there first.

I had a fern named Amelia in my room that I had watered on the day he died. I didn't water her again. Every day a few more brown leaves fell to the floor. At first I kept a record of how many leaves fell each day but then there were too many. I was very careful to leave them exactly where they fell.

I am a good student. I was on the dean's list every semester except my first one and I had an academic honors scholarship that paid a third of my tuition. This is not bragging it is just the truth. I do not have many friends but I will make up for it later by having a lot of money. I know that when the girls at work go to the Brass Monkey without inviting me they do it because they are jealous. Not that I would actually go drinking but they could invite me and I would very nonjudgmentally decline. I am also quite pretty, although usually I hide it.

I was taking Victorian poetry and Introduction to Legal Studies. I made an A and a B+, 3.65 average and the B+ was my father's fault. I am going to be a very wealthy lawyer. Very few people recognize my potential. Sometimes when I am on the elevator and the other people are ignoring me I think if only you knew who you are with. Someday I will be famous and you will never even know how close you were to me. And I feel sorry for them.

I do not feel sorry for Amelia. She should have been able to hold up longer than that. If you don't have any spunk you can't make it. I have wells of strength deep within me.

Malone is the only one who sees that now. He sees in me potential for greatness and I see it in him. My father did not like Malone but that is because he didn't understand. His eyes were blinded by his devotion to the religion of Christ instead of to Christ himself. Malone sees and helps me to see that Christ came to set us free, not to restrain us. My highest calling is to be a helpmeet for him, to obey him, to submit my desires to his, since only in losing my life shall I find it. Someday Malone will be very rich.

When I say that I am very strong I don't mean in every way. Only some. For example I am long-suffering. I can endure a lot of punishment when I know it will pay off later. Even if it's much later. I am patient. Malone hates having to be gone so much and loves me for quitting school to take this job but I don't mind I will make it pay off later. Delayed gratification. But I do not like confrontation. I have never said to Malone's mother you are driving me crazy leave me alone.

She has her own key to our apartment. Sometimes last night for example I come home from work and the table is set and dinner is in the oven and she is sitting on my sofa reading my newspaper and I want to scream. I hate it when she loads the dishwasher with the glasses on the bottom so that I will have to rearrange everything later. She has a twenty-year-old dishwasher from when they loaded glasses on the bottom and she just can't get it through her head that now you load them on the top.

I feel closer to Malone's family than I do to my mother and she is my only family. I have a grandmother but she lives in an institution in Iowa. My mother had a hysterectomy after I was born. When I was thirteen I heard her tell her friend be glad it happened now when I was pregnant you couldn't get one believe me I tried.

I believe that the sins of the fathers shall be visited on their children. My great-grandfather made a lot of money off of World War I and invested it all in a business supplies company. My grandfather married right out of college, joined the family business, bought a big house, and had a baby. The depression hit Alabama in 1928 and they lost everything. They took their hunting rifles, went out in the woods, and shot each other. Nobody knows if it was a suicide pact where they counted to three and shot each other or a double murder. Just that the father shot the son and the son shot the father.

If I had to kill myself or somebody else it would not be bloody. You can stick a nail in somebody's ear when they're asleep and they won't be able to figure out what did it if you pull it back out. A gas leak when they're asleep is also a good idea because it looks like an accident and doesn't leave a mess. I would never use a gun or a knife. I am against violence.

Malone is not.

If you do the nail you should probably give them sleeping pills too because if you accidentally woke them up how would you explain.

chapter 2

On my way to work every morning I predict how many phone messages for Mr. Brooks and how many for Mr. Ballard I will take that day. I can never guess the same numbers twice in one week. When I get there I fill out the top part of that number of message sheets for each lawyer and put my initials at the bottom. I always write the day then the month instead of the month then the day. If one of them gets more than my predicted number of messages in a day I cannot fill out the top part on them. They are trying to break me of this habit but what they don't realize is that in certain ways I cannot be broken. If they get less than I predicted I tear the leftover message sheets off the pad and take them home and put them in a box. In one month I have brought home eighteen empty message sheets, but fewer the last two weeks than the first. I have never torn the paper while I was tearing it off the pad. That is how they write dates in Europe. Most people think I've been to Europe.

On my way home sometimes I think about what happened that day. Sometimes I record my thoughts. Sometimes I just drive I try not to think.

Many people depend on me. If you see a powerful man look behind him and there's a woman. Women really run the world.

Malone for example. He wanted to go to seminary which shows how spiritual he really is but I knew he shouldn't. I have known people who went there. You study all that time and you end up not knowing any more answers. Just bigger questions. It had nothing to do with the fact that dentists make more money.

And my father. With my mother it's surprising he did as well as he did. I do not believe that he died in debt. Malone says we have to pray for her. I think we should take her to court. One way or another I will get my inheritance. This is an example of how determined I can be.

Today is our one-month wedding anniversary. During that time we have had sex eight times. I have faked three orgasms and actually had one. I will keep a record until our one-year anniversary and then I will stop.

After taxes I make $948.50 a month. This is our monthly budget:

Rent	$325
Utilities (Gas, Electricity, Phone)	$125
Food	$200
Tithe	$ 94.85
Car Payments	$269
Clothes	$ 50
School Supplies	$ 75

Entertainment	$ 40
Gasoline	$ 35
Miscellaneous	$100

Which means that until I get my inheritance we operate at a monthly deficit of $365.35 a month.

When Malone turns twenty-five he gets $100,000 that his grandfather left him. He has a government loan for tuition and the extra living expenses but I would rather pay for it with my inheritance so that I can get bigger alimony payments if we get divorced. I tried to get the loan in my name but I couldn't. I will never file for divorce because you can only get married again if your husband leaves you.

chapter 3

I used to have four invisible friends until I got tired of them and we went to the beach and I threw them in the ocean. None of them could swim.

I wish I could do that to God. I think He is real because I feel Him and sometimes I know He tries to keep me from doing what I want to do. He is very smart. I can do what I want to do anyway but I know that He sees me do it. The good thing about it is how when other people believe in Him they quit thinking for themselves. They become sheep. The Bible shows you how to manipulate them. I read it every night.

God is there when we have sex.

He wants me to talk to it. He says its name is Oney and if I kiss it it will turn into Boney. I just can't do it. When we wake up in the morning he says I should lick it. It makes me feel like throwing up.

Now we have had married sex nine times. Angie, another secretary at work, loaned me a book she was reading that she said was great so I read it and a girl in it had an orgasm actually many orgasms which were nothing like mine so I don't know if I ever have but I think it was wrong of me to read that book because I believe clean body, clean house, clean mind and I have asked God to forgive me. Angie is a bad influence she is pro-abortion and I don't think I will be friends with her anymore.

I know that I ought to let him do it whenever he wants because the Bible says but I put my foot down on Sundays. I spend Sundays at church with his mother, who does not like my mother because of what she has done to me.

I have not spoken to my mother in twenty-four days.

The day before Malone went to register for dental school he said *I wish you would help me more with this.* And I said I'll help what do you want. And he said *don't make me ask for it again because I hate to it's just that if we could use the money your daddy left you then we wouldn't have to go into debt to pay tuition because debt is unscriptural and of course I want to buy you some insurance and things and you just sure could make things a whole lot easier.* I said Malone I thought we discussed all this yesterday Mama said Daddy didn't leave anybody anything but debt. He said *I just don't see how that's legally possible your daddy lived in the same house for almost twenty years so it has to be paid off or almost anyway and the barbershop was doing fine he had to be worth a lot of money and if nothing else at least he had life insurance.* Which I hated him temporarily for bringing up although I never let the sun go down on my anger and I said well I don't understand it either and what is legally possible supposed to mean but that's the way it is and anyway you were planning to get a loan before we got married and we can pay it back in two years when you get your grandfather's money. And he said *well I'd think you would have a little more loyalty to your husband than that you sound like you married me for my money which by the way if I didn't have to use for tuition I could use to set up a practice did you ever think about that.* While he said that about the practice I said as loud as I could you shut up I did no such thing which was unusual for me I am not the type of person to say shut up. But he didn't he said *I just think it's a little bit funny that your mama can go and sell the Chevrolet which should have been ours and keep all that money when we're the ones who need it and deserve it but you put her selfishness before my needs thanks a lot for being there for me.* And grabbed the teeth on the coffee table and threw them in his book bag and left.

That night when his mother picked me up for our LIFE group (Ladies' Intensive Fellowship and Evangelism) she told me *you're just the sweetest little thing and God knows I hope Malone stays as loyal to me as you are to your mama but you got your own family now and you got to stand up for what's right the Bible says to be a good steward with your money and you shouldn't let your mama squander it all when your own family is in need just because she has given her mind over to the devil and become possessed by selfishness.* I said I never thought about it like that. And she said *that's because you have such a kind heart but you got to remember that you got legal rights and even the Lord won't stand for people taking what's not theirs and for your mama's sake as well as for your own you can't let that happen.*

The more I thought about it the madder I got—mad at Malone for accusing me of all that and mad at my mama for cheating me out of that money and mad at Malone's mama for always butting in and mad at my daddy for causing all this to happen in the first place. So as soon as I get home I slam the door and I say Malone we have to talk and I'm ready to let him have it only he's not home. So I walk straight over to the kitchen phone and dial my mama's number and I say all right I have had it Daddy's dying is hard on all of us but you can't use it as an excuse to steal money from your own daughter so you can just write me a check for everything that I've got coming to me and put it in the mail tomorrow morning. *Sweetheart we have to talk about this.* Not now Mother I don't have the energy for another argument with you. And hung up.

There's nothing wrong with standing up for yourself I don't feel guilty for claiming what's mine. You don't have to be a wimp just because you're a Christian. People always think of Jesus as some emaciated little nerd with no chest hair but He was a carpenter before they had power tools which would take muscles plus think of overturning the moneychangers' table in the temple.

I have never hung up on my mother before what is happening to me.

When Malone got home he came in the bedroom and I woke up and I said turn on the lights and he did and I sat up and looked at him and as soon as my eyes worked I said all right Malone I did it I called her I hope you're happy because I'm not going to be talked to like you talked to me before. And it worked. He sat on the edge of the bed with his back to me and looked at the floor and said very slowly *I don't know why I said all that I didn't mean it* at least I think that's what he said he said it so quietly you could hardly hear. And I'm not that easy I said well why did you say it Malone I need some answers. And he started taking off his shoes and he said *I don't know maybe it's just that I'm under a lot of pressure right now* and I let out a half cough half sigh like I was frustrated which I was because who isn't and he said *okay I won't make excuses I'm just sorry.* I didn't say anything I was the strong silent type. *I don't know what to say I'm so sorry* looking at his shoes all that time and then he turned towards me practically crying I mean tears in his eyes and his voice cracking saying *I do love you I don't know what comes over me but when things go bad at school something snaps inside me sometimes and it's like it makes me try to drive away all the best parts of my life I don't understand why myself there's just something horrible inside me* his hands very tense you could see all the finger bones up to the wrist and blood veins all the way up his arms. So I touched his elbow sometimes it takes more strength to forgive somebody than to stay mad plus you always have to think of that crown and I said no there isn't I didn't mean to say that you're horrible. *Yes I am there's something horrible that makes me do the exact opposite of what I want to do.* Not all the time you don't Malone. *Please don't ever leave me I deserve for you to leave me but I'm sorry and I mean it you're the very best thing that ever happened to me and I promise I'll never speak to you that way again I'll always be good to you.* And we both held each other very tight. I'll never leave you.

Which I won't. Marriage is sacred if you get divorced it is a sin. It is the world's answer not God's. I live in this world not of it.

The next morning the alarm rang and he reached over me to turn it off and put his arm around me and said *let's make a totally new start today and I promise I'll never be that way again.* I said I know. *I mean it if you don't think there is any money just drop it we'll get by.* And I said no you were right we owe it to ourselves to find out and I will. And he kissed me and I held my breath so he wouldn't smell morning breath.

15

chapter 4

I got to work late today. Angie said *were you in a wreck*. I said no I'm so stupid I just closed my finger in the car door last night and broke it. She said *what about your eye*. I said my finger hurt so bad I hit my eye. She looked at me funny. I looked at her not funny. She better mind her own business. I can't type for three to four weeks so I do Angie's filing and answer the phone more and she does my typing. I wish I were better with makeup. And I wish all the people who don't give a shit about me would stop affecting concern.

Malone is right about one thing. I am going to have

to start watching my language. But I think you're also taking the Lord's name in vain if you say something like the Lord led me to do something you just want to do anyway but you think saying that makes it sound better. For example almost every time Malone's mother decides to butt in she starts by saying I was interceding for you in prayer and the Lord laid it on my heart to come talk to you about this.

I couldn't sleep again last night.

My nightgown gets all bunched up around my stomach and I just lie there listening to Malone breathe. Sometimes I try to breathe with him but I practically suffocate he breathes so slow. When he starts to snore I try to make him roll over but I can't.

If you mess with him too much while he's asleep he'll roll over and drop his arm on your face which will hurt.

I do not buy sleeping pills for three reasons:

1. They are expensive.
2. My Uncle Dwight, whom I hate, is an alcoholic, and I'm afraid addictive behavior runs in the family.
3. If I ever kill myself I'm leaning toward sleeping pills.

Suicide is a sin but not a mortal sin. Sometimes you have to lose your life to find it. For example Judas I think he is in Heaven because he followed Jesus up until the end and then he got out of fellowship but then he felt so sorry that that was the only way he could show God how sorry he was which takes a certain kind of strength courage. I would be more worried about him if he hadn't done it.

I wouldn't do it if I could just get this money from my mother. All this because of the money.

He said *did you go to the bank today*. I said yes. He said *good because I need fifty dollars for school* and reached in my purse. I said for what not because I didn't hear but because I couldn't believe and it makes me nervous when he goes in my purse and I was hoping he would stop to answer me but he didn't he just kept fishing around in there while he was talking. He said *books are expensive but I don't see the point of going to dental school if I'm not going to buy the books dammit*. Okay but you bought a thirty-dollar book last week and that money is our grocery money for the whole week. He got two twenties out all I had and threw my purse on the floor *get off my back we'll just eat at my mother's this week since she for one is willing to help me*. Go ahead and say it all this is my mother's fault. *You can blame it on your mother if that makes you feel better*. It's not my fault Malone god damn it I hate her I absolutely hate her she's practically ruining my marriage. *Shut up I don't want to hear that kind of language in my house you bitch* grabbing me so hard I had to scream stop it you're hurting me and I pushed him away. Then he stepped back and looked at me like I was a leper and said *I don't know what has happened to you*. I don't know what's happened to both of us and I sat down on the sofa and stared at the roach motel in the corner. *Well I do I'm sure as hell that you're the one causing our problems because God is punishing you for some kind of attitude problem you've got and I'm an innocent bystander who has to suffer because of the fallout of God's wrath on you*. Malone. *Well I'm just going to have to pray for God to straighten out you and your mama it's all I can do*. What do you want me to do sue my own mama. *I wash my hands of the whole thing how about you just go to God and repent and do whatever He tells you to fix things* picking up his book bag and slinging it over his shoulder. Wait answer me do you want me to sue her. *I've said my say*. And slammed the door behind him.

And now I have to pay for my finger which I can't do and I hate to bring it up to Malone but he bought our insurance through the school and I don't know who the company is or how to contact them so I'll have to. What a bastard. I'm telling you this is serious I am a child of God and God is not going to put up with him treating me like this.

I took two aspirin and waited a half hour until I couldn't stand up it hurt so bad so then I went to the hospital and

I had to drive myself which shows something like I can rise to a crisis and I said please help me. They said *what's the name of your insurance company*. And I said I don't know but it's through the university whatever their student insurance company is because my husband is a student. *That's not enough we have to have a name if we're going to bill it through them.* So I said call my husband he's at home and I gave them the number, all this while I'm sitting there with a broken finger throbbing all the way up my arm into my head and there's all these disgusting bloody people around me and germs everywhere and they come back in about fifteen minutes by my watch which felt like two hours. *Your husband isn't home.* Oh yeah he had to go to the library can't you do something if I sign in blood that you'll get your damn money. And they said *what's your yearly income*. And I told them. And they said *do you have anyone who can verify that*. And I told them to call Mr. Hampton Brooks which I guess they did because they came back twenty minutes later and said *we'll just send the bill to you and you can work it out with your insurance company*. I said fine why don't you do something that you can charge me for you idiot. *We are working as fast as we can but we've had three attempted suicides tonight and they have priority over broken fingers.* I said did they have insurance but the nurse walked away like she didn't hear.

19

When I finally got to see a doctor he acted like I was five years old and said *now how did this happen*. And I said I don't know it was just an accident. He said *what were we doing*. I said if it's any of your business I was playing touch football and I fell but I thought about saying we were playing football and we fell. *We're going to have to be more careful.* Did we save those attempted suicides. *Those weren't my cases.* I waited out there over two and a half hours because you had three attempted suicides and you didn't even have them. *When one doctor gets a case like that the others have to cover for him and it slows things up but I'm very sorry if you were inconvenienced.* I said how did they do it. Because I'm thinking I don't want to be rushed to the hospital and saved by some doctor who thinks of me as the case that slowed things up and talked about as the source of inconvenience for people with broken fingers and maybe if they get me at a certain time I'll live but I'll be brain-damaged and too stupid to try again and they'll put me in a nuthouse and university students will go on tours of it and look at me like I'm a mental patient.

I went on a tour like that once with my psych class and had a conversation with a schizophrenic and I kept thinking this is a very interesting person who hears interesting voices and maybe they really are angels like he says but maybe they're demons and he's demon-possessed and he seems nice because Satan is trying to tempt me by wearing a cloak of light and maybe he wants to rape me.

So as I leave the hospital they hand me a bill for $134 and I can take a lot but you reach a point where you're not going to take any more and I had reached mine. I didn't even look at it. I just walked out the door.

I didn't read it until today and I called them up and I say what in hell do you think you're doing charging me $134 for one broken finger when all you did was tie it to a metal stick I mean you didn't even put a cast on it. And the woman said *can I have your name please.* I told her. *Address please.* I told her. *Insurance company.* I forgot to ask my husband. *Well I can't do anything until I know the name of your insurance company.* You can't even tell me what this bill is for. *Well apparently you broke your finger.* I know that much is there anyone more intelligent that I could talk to. *No there isn't.* Okay see if you can understand this I would like to know exactly what this one-hundred-and-thirty-four-dollar bill is for. *You would like an itemized bill.* Yes. *Hold please.* So I'm on hold for fifteen minutes and then she comes back. *Are you still there.* Yes I've been here the whole time. *Here are your itemized expenses:*

> *Emergency room* $40

Do you mean that you charged me rent to sit there in that germ-infested room where I probably caught AIDS or malaria and wait for two and a half hours. *That's just the standard emergency room charge for anyone who gets treated there.* Well that sucks.

Doctor's exam	37
X ray	27
Bandages	17
Miscellaneous	13

What the hell is miscellaneous did I buy drinks for all the nurses who poked at me. *It might be painkiller I don't know that expense is not explained in the accounting department's file.* Well I should have gone into medical accounting you people have got some kind of racket going. And hung up.

On my way to work today I went to Eckerd's for some painkiller and saw these metal splints on sale for $2.98 which makes me pretty mad about the $17. When I got home I got a $20 bill from the doctor who interpreted my X ray they don't waste a second when it comes to sending out bills. I saw the X ray and it did not take $20 to look at it and see a crack. If I get another bill tomorrow I'm going to tear it up. I'm going to have to tell Malone.

So we are going through a tough time but I will get through it I will come out stronger. I count it all joy my brothers when I experience various trials knowing that the testing of my faith produces endurance and let endurance have its perfect result that you may be perfect and complete lacking in nothing. Malone just better realize that there is a limit to God's patience. If you do something to the least of these you do it to Christ and He won't take much more of this.

I still haven't decided but I have ruled out anything painful including:

1. AIDS.
2. Any kind of gun.
3. Slitting wrists.

4. Jumping off something.
5. Car crash.

I never tell any of this to anyone. I only make these tapes when I'm alone in the car or when Malone is asleep or in the lab. I am not crazy but some people might think so if they knew me better. If I didn't do this I don't know whether I would go crazy or not. Malone is the one people should worry about. Dental school is more pressure than we thought.

6. Fire.

chapter 5

I was not kidding about Malone. He needs help. Worse than
I do.

I'm serious I think he is cracking up I am really scared.
When he came home tonight his eyes were all strange he
walked and talked strange he even smelled strange. I mean
I thought about trying to cast demons out of him it was so
strange.

There was this knock on the door like somebody knocked
up against it and I thought who in the world and I turned
off the TV and even though I thought who in the world I
knew exactly who it was. I could just feel it. So I went to
open the door and on the way to the door I was thinking

reunion I was thinking of Scarlett and Rhett when he came back he's a scoundrel like Rhett Butler but I know what he needs and I can give it to him deep down I am the only woman for him what a fool I was. But when I got to the door and opened it he opened it with his key at the same time and we just stood there I couldn't say anything I couldn't even think anything. I should have said frankly Malone I don't give a damn and slammed the door in his face. But I didn't I just said oh it's you. And he said *what are you doing here*. I live here. He said *where were you last night*. Where were you. *Can I come in*. You live here too. And he looked at my hand and his hands started shaking I don't know he looked like he was about to cry his face was all red. So I said come in and I felt like I'd never seen him before. I just looked at his face and his eyes and his hair and I thought who in the world are you and how could I have ever had sex with you and I was just watching him like he was a movie studying him. And he went over to the sofa and sat down and put his elbows on his legs and put his forehead in the palms of his hands and shook his head back and forth which in that position makes your whole body sway. And the strangest thing was I wasn't thinking are you back are we going to make up now do you still want me do I still want you I was thinking who is this person I mean who is he really. And I looked at his hair just looked at it like it was under a microscope meaning that's all I saw and I thought of how I would describe it if I ever had to describe it to the police. It is the color of dog mess but I wouldn't say that I would say it is the color of this table somewhere between the color of this table and the color of pumpernickel bread. That's what I was thinking about I was standing with my hand on the doorknob thinking about his hair. And then he said so softly I could barely hear him *I'm sorry I'm so sorry I'm sorry I'm so sorry* and he kept saying it it practically turned into a chant and all the man went out of his voice he sounded like a little girl. He would sway to the left and say *I'm sorry* and sway to the right and say *I'm so sorry* he was still in that position. And I don't know why I didn't even think of comforting him I just watched and listened to this ambulance from far away get nearer and nearer then a little farther away and stop at the hospital. I didn't even care. I just stood there and didn't move a muscle. And then I started thinking about the irony of him being here cracking up and me not even caring after all we've been through and he's just going *I'm sorry I'm so sorry* and I'm just watching observing. And after we've done this for about fifteen minutes which when you're doing this is a long time I went in the bathroom and out of the blue threw up what a night and when I came back out he was sound asleep or passed out on the sofa.

So I don't know what to do. I mean I can't go to Mother's after what I said to her but I don't think I should wake him up. Ambulance sirens scream outside our window. I feel like **25** yelling shut up leave us alone is it always this way.

Sometimes I think he is on drugs or going insane what he is doing is not normal. And I don't know if you should let them sleep it off or what but I don't think you should make them mad for your own good. I wasn't serious about the police drugs are against the law and I am against drugs just say no but I didn't want to call the police and invite them to raid my apartment who knows he may have drugs hidden right here in the flour in the sofa wherever and I would call the police to get rid of him and I end up getting thrown in jail for possession no thank you. I can't believe I actually think my own husband might be on drugs but I do.

Isn't that the way to solve everything. I fell asleep hunched over the kitchen table and when I woke up he was gone. He is a pain in the neck. Literally.

chapter 6

Okay that was wrong I always admit it when I'm wrong. I mean I think it's important to be patient and forgiving but not to be a wimp if the other person isn't sorry but Malone really was is so I have to forgive him. So I do.

If maybe there is a small part of you that doesn't want to forgive somebody then you have to ask God to help you. Think about praying forgive us as we forgive our debtors judge not lest ye be not judged that should help and then you just say no matter what I feel I forgive seventy times seven which is not 490 it just means however many times you think is reasonable to forgive somebody forgive them seventy times that many. And then you just do it you don't live by your feelings. A Christian should never say under the circumstances I feel whatever because he should always rise above circumstances.

Plus this is not what he's really like. When someone else is having a problem like me when Daddy died he'll be there for them like that. He came over that night and gave me a rose and he said *I want to be here for you I know how you feel I love you* that was the first time he had ever told me that and he meant it he had tears in his eyes and he stayed with me through what was a very hard time for me and I just knew he was sent from the Lord to comfort me like He takes one person and gives me another. He can be very compassionate and sensitive and maybe he doesn't show it right this minute but he will again. He is under a lot of stress right now and he needs me to be strong for him. He **27** was there for me and now I will stay here for him. I just have to be patient and wait and pray. What else can I do.

When I got home from work today he was making dinner and the table was set with candles. And I just looked at it and I said thanks. And he said *can you ever forgive me.* I have to admit I was still mad because obviously but I said okay and I was still mad sort of but I believe forgiveness is like love it is not a feeling it is a commitment. He said *I'm sorry I promise I'll never hurt you again* and you have to know him when he is that sorry for something you can't stay mad that long he has big brown eyes and long eyelashes like a cow and he can be so sweet and he said *tonight is your pamper night* and he brought me my bear-claw slippers and put them on my feet you've never seen anyone so gentle and tender. I said Malone you don't have to do all this because he really was sorry the sorriest I've ever seen anybody and it's a med-ical fact that stress will make you do weird things so I was feeling better. And he said *I know I just want to show you how much I love you.* I love you too. *And I need you I need you so badly if it wasn't for you I would have dropped out of dental school by now and become a total nothing.* No you wouldn't. *Yes I would and I promise I'm going to make it up to you when I get out I'm going to buy you a big house in Mountain Brook and we'll have a maid and anything you want.* Stop it Malone it's okay.

Everything is fine now and God is taking so much care to build my character that I just know He is preparing me for something very special whom the Lord loves He chastises. And I am not going to think morbid sinful thoughts anymore and we are going to read the Bible together every night. We have been brought through fire and now we are shining and pure.

chapter 1

Okay we got off to a bad start but we are starting over new life in Christ and now our motto is love joy peace patience kindness gentleness self-control.

I will be a good wife. I will be a good daughter-in-law. I will be a good secretary.

I am not a good daughter. I can't be a good daughter and sue my mama and I can't be a good wife and not.

I am a very good secretary. I am a loving joyful peaceful patient kind gentle self-controlled secretary.

I am in charge of the plants in Mr. Brooks's and Mr. Ballard's offices and the one on my desk. I like to keep Mr. Brooks's on the verge between life and death, which is not easy because if it goes too far over the line he will have it thrown out and I will have to start over. He will not wait until it is actually dead. So I keep it too sick to look good and too well to be thrown out. It's easier with Mr. Ballard but not as fun because he wouldn't notice if his plant coughed and fell over dead right in front of him. He has the world's messiest office and when he asked me to find something the other day I said Mr. Ballard you think I'm going into the eye of a hurricane to find a will that I'm not even named in. He didn't laugh he said *just find it.* I take care of my plant like she was a baby.

If I was in charge of Mr. Jackson's plant I would take very good care of it. He is a new attorney who would show a lot more interest in me if I weren't married. He is very nice.

I am sort of sorry about Amelia. Sometimes I am afraid something terrible will happen to me because of what I did to her.

I made a mark in the book when the phone rang.

> *Dark house, by which once more I stand*
> *Here in the long unlovely street,*
> *Doors where my heart was used to beat*
> *So quickly, waiting*

Hello.

. . . *He is dead.*

Mama?

Irwin is dead.

Mama? What happened? Where are you?

He died. I'm in the hotel but I'm taking a flight home tonight. I want you to arrange to be home by tomorrow afternoon.

Mother what happened to Daddy?

They think he killed himself. I guess it was worse than we thought. They're going to do an autopsy.

Mama pull yourself together. Daddy would not kill himself. I'm sure they have him confused with somebody else.

I just identified the body.

. . . Oh God. . . . How?

Drowned. Listen. I can't talk any more. Just go home.

I don't have many black summer clothes. This is what I packed:

1. My four nicest outfits:
   a. Pink striped dress with dropped waist.
   b. Blue and grey plaid skirt and top.
   c. White skirt with blue and peach cotton sweater.
   d. Black striped skirt and black rayon sweater.
2. My six best panties.
3. My three best bras.
4. My two best slips.
5. My yellow flowered nightgown.
6. Hose. I don't have enough hose but I will take some of hers.
7. Toothbrush. Toothpaste.
8. Makeup. Deodorant.
9. White flats.
10. Black pumps.
11. Books.

31

That was one of the best packing jobs I ever did. When I arrived nothing was wrinkled. Malone helped.

The preacher was at our house all the time while I was there and I kept wondering what does he think he is doing here because no one invited him but people think if they are doing something for the Lord they don't need manners.

People will wonder do you think the mother or the daughter will be next that kind of thing runs in families. Will she have to drop out of school I heard it was financial trouble. Really I heard the marriage had gone sour probably a combination.

I wonder why I didn't do what he wanted. Where he is. How they got him home for the funeral. What she has done to him.

I keep thinking about the $57.53. I had $57.53 in my savings account and he called me one day at school and said I took the $57.53 out of your account because I just think you ought to help pay for your own education and I didn't care I just thought why didn't you ask me first.

After the autopsy we found out about the heart attack but most people didn't.

I'm not so sure about drowning. I've heard it can make you look bloated but I think that's only if nobody pulls you out soon enough. There's no guarantee because if you go where they can pull you out before you get bloated they might do it too soon. I don't want any physical change. I want to look beautiful. There is something wonderful about a beautiful young woman who is dead. I saw a soap opera once where a girl mixed some herbal tea that gave her a heart attack and they couldn't figure out if she had meant to. I think the writers must have been high when they wrote that I never watch soap operas I was just changing the channel. I'm not too sure about sleeping pills anymore either because what if I threw them up. I hate to throw up worse than anything. The other thing is I hate the thought of them taking off my clothes and cutting me open and looking anywhere they want. I want to put on my own makeup and fix my own hair and choose my own outfit and not be fooled with. My house will be clean at the time. I could leave a note saying this is how I did it believe me so don't cut me open but I'm not sure that would stop them. I know about lungs and drowning but I wonder what's different about a heart with a heart attack.

chapter 2

Love is not a feeling. It's a commitment.

And I am totally committed to Malone it's not that it's just that he has changed so much. Not to dwell in the past but when we first started dating he was just so different. He never drank he hardly ever got mad and when he did it was never at me he is a passionate person that's all. He is also very smart. He didn't make such great grades in college because he didn't go to a very good high school and didn't know how to study but his senior year which is when we started dating we studied together I told him you have to discipline yourself you have to do it every day heartily as unto the Lord and he started doing much better good enough

to get accepted into dental school which is no small potatoes. I can do so much for him I can make him very successful
if he'll just let me if he'll just realize how much he needs
me which he will if I just hang in there long enough good
will ultimately triumph.

When I started dating Malone I was the only one who
saw his potential and I'm not saying I went into this blindly
I knew what people thought but I also saw more than they
saw I have the gift of seeing other people's potential. The
girls on my hall all started gossiping about it and two of
them even came to my room just to tell me *you're just asking*
for trouble if you stay with him. And I didn't know how to
explain the whole thing I just said you don't understand him
he is a very misunderstood person. *We understand him perfectly*
that's why we're saying what we're saying like for one thing he has a
bad temper. I know that and he knows that but he wants me
to help him work on it and I couldn't explain that he helps
me too I want to be a godly woman and Malone helps me
develop character and if you are a Christian and somebody
needs you you just can't turn your back on them because
it's not convenient to help them what if Christ had done
that but I couldn't explain all that. *How can you help him work*
on that. I don't know exactly just be there let him know he
can count on me see he has all this anger inside of him
because he's afraid of being deserted but he's learning to
redirect it into something positive he needs me. They didn't
get it their eyes were blinded in the way they were trying
to blind me by self-interest. It's still true though if I ever
teach him to redirect that anger into something positive he
will be a great man.

Mother didn't understand him either she said *what is*
wrong with you do you have some sort of masochistic compulsion. No
I don't don't say such a horrible thing. *What is it then you had*
such a sweet and loving father such a good man and yet you are
attracted to this angry abusive messed up kid which wasn't fair she
didn't give him a chance. And I told her Mother Malone
isn't perfect and he's not a kid but I don't want somebody
who is perfect think of Uncle Dwight why do you still let

Uncle Dwight stay with you when he's trying to dry out after everything that's happened because he needs you that's why well Malone needs me and I'm making a difference in his life I'm helping him. *Well he's making a difference in your life too but it's a bad difference.* No it isn't Mother I don't expect you to understand this but I am becoming a better person a deeper person because I'm developing a patient long-suffering forgiving spirit I'm learning how to love unconditionally like Christ loves the Church and that's important to me. And she just looked at me and finally said *you are a beautiful person and you deserve somebody who will treat you with dignity and respect.* Well I have found that person it's Malone. She shook her head she was mad and she went in her room and closed the door but if her eyes are blinded to anybody who does things a little differently that's her problem not mine I don't have to listen to that I take orders from God **35** not her and I know that God wants me with Malone.

Malone is a survivor and so am I that is one reason we go together. If you have been abused in some way as a child you have to either grow up to be an abuser or continue to be abused or develop a thick skin I heard this on *Oprah Winfrey* and we both have thick skin. His grandfather knew his father wasn't any good, which is why he left the money to Malone.

So I am Malone's number one supporter and I am not being judgmental or not supportive when I say this but I am not stupid either I know right from wrong and I know if I were in dental school I wouldn't have to go out on weekends and get drunk. Getting drunk is a sin. The Bible says plain as day.

I think this has to do with him feeling inadequate because he feels he is not being a good provider like his masculinity is threatened so I try hard not to say anything about where does our money go. I know if I could just get that money. But I do wonder. Last time our bank statement came there were four William Teller withdrawals of fifty dollars each. And if I ask him he overreacts and says *who is head of this house anyway do I have to ask for your permission every time I need something.* Which he is trying to reach out for help saying he cares so much and wants to take care of me and he needs me to believe in him and when I ask he feels like I'm saying you're not doing your job. So I said that's not what I'm saying. And he said *and maybe that money is our tithe money did you ever think of that* because he is in charge of that. I said is it. He said *the Bible says don't let your right hand know what your left hand is doing so I don't want to talk about it but I'll tell you one thing I don't think it's right of you to criticize me for giving money to the Lord when you are closing your eyes to the fact that your mama is hoarding our money just because she goes through the charade of saying that she is in debt well I for one don't feel one bit sorry for her and if she is having a little trouble so what it's not like everybody else in the world hasn't had to balance a checkbook at one time or another.* Stop it Malone what do you want me to do I have done everything I can think of. *Except one.* Just shut up. So I don't ask but I am afraid because if he doesn't tell me we are going to overdraw so I just always try to leave $100 in the account in case he does that but I hardly can.

I don't know what has driven him to the friends he has but I know one thing they are bad people. Sometimes I think I should pray for them but I think I hate them. They are wild and I think they have been to prostitutes. They are a bad influence on Malone and they take him out drinking which costs a lot of money and sometimes I think they do drugs. Rusty and Claire are the worst. They come over at 1:00 or 2:00 in the morning and walk in our bedroom and pull Malone out of bed to go drinking with them. Malone gave them a key because we live so close to campus he said *they might need to come over and go to the bathroom* (He didn't say it like that. He has started using crude language around me. Actually he said *shit.*) *or take a nap.* I said if I come home in the middle of the day I don't want some strange person in my bed. He said *don't come home in the middle of the day then and don't be so selfish don't you think the Lord would want you to share.*

Sometimes when Malone talks about God I hate Him.

I hate it when people talk about the Lord only they

say the Lard. His mother does that all the time. Malone says Lard only when he is mad or drunk.

I just think all this is related to the money. And maybe God is punishing me. I didn't marry Malone because of the $100,000 I really didn't because I didn't even know about it when we first started dating but then I thought about it a lot it is a lot of money. And then when my father died and I didn't think we had any money I thought I'm going to have to drop out of school and never go back and always be a secretary and then I will never be rich and famous and the girls down the hall will never be sorry but if I marry him then when he gets out of dental school he will owe it to me to let me go back to college and then law school. And then right after we got married Malone figured out about my inheritance and I realized I didn't need him after all but I believe that marriage is sacred and that divorce is **37** a sin so I never even thought about that.

chapter 3

My mother called me at work today. I said Mother what do you want this is the last thing I need. She said *sweetheart I want to put this thing behind us I want to have some peace between us tell me how you're doing.* And I said well I've got a broken finger and I can't afford to pay the doctor but nothing that would concern you. She said *you poor thing how did it happen.* I said somebody dropped something on it at work. *That's just horrible but maybe your firm would pay for it.* You'd like that wouldn't you but they won't. *Oh that's too bad.* Mother don't act like you're concerned when you're not. *But I am.* Does this mean you're going to give me my money. *I don't have any of your money.* Mother we've had this conversation a hundred times

I know what you're going to say and you know what I'm going to say I know you think you've got problems but believe me I've got them too. *Okay I can see you're not ready for a reconciliation but I do have to ask your advice about something so I'll get right to it how do I go about looking for a job.* Oh Mother this is low even for you I'm not going to close my eyes to the fact that you are hoarding Daddy's money just because you go through the charade of saying that you need a job and I'm not going to feel sorry for you either if you have to work it's not like everybody else in the world doesn't have to. *I'm not asking.* Well this is the last straw Mother if you don't want to give me my money then I have no choice but to sue dammit. *Don't let me hear you talk like that.* You won't have to anymore. And hung up.

So I am going to ask Mr. Jackson what to do about my mother. I think Mr. Brooks or Mr. Ballard would charge me **39** because it is firm policy but if I could just get Mr. Jackson alone and explain he would do it for free. I will try to do that before I talk to Malone about the hospital bills.

Tonight when Malone got home from the lab I said can we talk. He said *don't ask me just talk* because he always gets grumpy when there's a low-pressure system in the air, or maybe high. I forget. And I said okay I've decided to ask Mr. Jackson how we can sue for the money. And he said *baby I'm so proud of you you don't know what this means to me* and he came over to me and hugged me. I don't know why but it made me feel like crying so I didn't say anything I just hugged him back and he felt strong and warm and good and we just stood there like that for a long time until I said I'm glad that makes you happy. He said *oh believe me it does this is such an answer to prayer and it tells me that now you think of me as your family instead of your mother which is the Christian way because God says a woman must leave her father and mother and cleave to her husband and I've been hurt for so long because I just didn't think you were doing that.* And then I was crying because I realized why all this had been happening and I said Malone I'm so sorry I've just been horrible. And he said *I'm sorry too and you know I'll always forgive you when you do something like this to show me that you've really repented.* You're so good to me. *I want you to know that I'm going to be there for you encouraging you every day to fight the good fight on this one because you have a Christian duty to stand up for what is rightfully ours and that this is the best way in the world for you to prove to me how much I mean to you.*

Since the last time I said which has been a month we have not had sex at all but I have still taken my pills. Which is a good thing because I think things will improve now.

chapter 4

I did it. I got to work this morning and filled out eighteen message sheets—eight for Mr. Brooks and ten for Mr. Ballard—watered my plant and Mr. Ballard's plant and went down the hall and knocked on Mr. Jackson's door. When he said come in I felt like throwing up because usually he doesn't get in until 9:00 or 9:30 and it wasn't even 8:30 so I didn't even have anything to say but when he said come in again I figured I have to do it so I may as well get it over with and I opened his door.

He is so good-looking. He went to the Bahamas two weeks ago and his nose is still peeling. He has this receding hairline which Angie says somehow on him looks sexy and his hair in the back is long for a lawyer it goes about halfway down his collar in little curls like if he grew it another inch or two and wore a smock he would look like a French artist. He also doesn't wear a wedding ring so Angie is determined to marry him. What a fool.

So anyway I said hi Mr. Jackson do you have a minute. He said *I'm preparing for a court appearance this afternoon but I can spare a minute* which shows how important and nice he is. I said well my father died not too long ago and I think my mother has sort of lost her mind temporarily or something but anyway she won't give me the money my father left me and I was wondering what you think I should do. He sat there thinking for about a minute and I started sweating and I thought oh I should never have asked just get me out of here what am I going to say now and then finally he said *like I said I've got this court appearance so today is pretty bad and I'll be out of town for the rest of the week but why don't you get the name of her lawyer for me and I'll make some phone calls and see if I can find something out for you next week.* I said oh Mr. Jackson this means so much to me I really appreciate it because he really is the nicest lawyer I have ever known but then I thought maybe I should say you aren't going to charge me for this are you but then I thought if I don't ask then maybe he won't but if I do maybe he'll remember that he is supposed to but before I actually decided he got up and walked me to the door and opened it for me because he is a real southern gentleman and said *no problem.* I bet he knows I am going to law school.

So when Malone got home tonight I told him and I had his favorite meal ready which is meatloaf baked potatoes and jello and fruit and we had a candlelight dinner to celebrate. He had some beer and I had some of Rusty's wine that was in our refrigerator which I rarely do but it was a special occasion. And he said *I just want you to know how sorry I am.* And I could think of a few things and I said for what. And he said *I'm under more pressure than I've ever been in my life and I need you so badly but I know I don't treat you right I'm just not good enough for you.* You are good enough for me I know what you're going through and that this isn't going to last as long as our love. And he kissed me and said *Little Poodle I don't deserve you but I promise I'm going to be better.* I said I'll be better too Mr. Bully. So I forgave him I really did and God will bless that.

Then he turned on some music and we cleaned up the dishes and I washed the kitchen floor and made a meatloaf sandwich to take to work tomorrow while he watched a *Dukes of Hazzard* rerun and then I said do you have to study tonight. And he said *I probably should but I'm so proud of you that I'd rather spend some time with you* which means he loves me but he is just not the type to say it all the time. So we watched TV together and I could just tell that God was blessing me for what I had done so I figured why spoil things and decided not to mention the medical bills for a few more days.

43

Then just as I predicted we had sex. During the human-interest story of the ten o'clock news which was about a Kinko's Copies store that burned down last night and destroyed some graduate student's dissertation notes that he had been working on for a year and a half and this morning he heard about the fire and ran down there in his pajama top and blue jeans and couldn't stop crying. They tried to interview him and he couldn't even talk. I wonder if he will kill himself.

I woke up when I dreamed that Malone was trying to kill me by pulling out all my teeth and came in here.

chapter 5

When we woke up this morning Malone said *what are you going to do today.* I said go to work and come home. He said *and.* I said and what. *Are you forgetting something.* Apparently. *Your mother's lawyer.* Oh yeah find out who Mother's lawyer is. *Good.* How do I do that. *How should I know* which meant you got us into this you get us out. I said I guess I'll just call her and ask her and turned on the TV.

So when I got to work I called her at home and just as I suspected she was just bluffing she didn't really get a job. I said Mother it's me. She said *oh I'm so glad to hear from you how are you.* The same Mother exactly the same. *Oh okay well can I do something for you.* The question is will you. *I will if I can* all the words staccato. Well can you tell me who your lawyer is. *Yes her name is Ann Barton she works at Smith, Habeth and Fornam* and I wrote that down. A woman. *Yes but I have to tell you that she'll send you a bill just for talking to you on the phone.* That doesn't scare me Mother. *Well I'm glad you're going to call her and I hope she'll be able to straighten all this out.* I think she will. I didn't tell her about Mr. Jackson because I figure he's like an ace up my sleeve and especially with a woman lawyer. I wish he were in town this week.

Malone's mother made dinner tonight so when she said she wanted to stay and eat with us I couldn't say no even though I hinted that since it's getting to be pretty close to finals Malone would get home who knows when so we might not eat until late because she thinks we always eat together but she said *oh I don't mind I'll wait plus that'll give us a chance to visit now tell me all about your law office.* So I told her about **45** what Mr. Jackson is going to do but nothing else about him and she said *praise the Lord you just watch He's going to honor you for this.* For some reason I never did tell her about Mama looking for a job or not having one when I called today I just said not much else is happening. She said *I wish I could get you involved in the church's Christmas bazaar.* I said I don't know. She said *it's always so much fun and almost all the ladies in the church do something so it's a great way to get to know people do you know many good Christian girls your own age.* Not really. *Well everybody could use some more friends.* Which I agree because without my mama I don't have anybody but all I said was yeah. And she said *I got it that's how He's going to bless you you just volunteer to make some goodies or man a booth or something and I bet you meet a real nice girl your age and you become great friends and maybe she'll have a husband Malone's age too.* I said that would be nice.

Malone got home about seven and was in a horrible mood so as it turned out I was glad she was there because he wouldn't do certain things in front of her. But it was the kind of bad mood that makes everybody else feel strange talking so we ate dinner without saying anything which was fine because I was tired of her and then Malone said *don't wait up* which means he won't be home and grabbed his book bag and left. She looked at me like is there anything you ought to tell me and I said finals and started clearing the table. She picked up Malone's plate and started to carry it over to the sink and I said don't bother with that I'll get it because I just wanted her to leave but no she cleans up her own mess so we did the dishes together even though the kitchen is too small for two people. Then I said boy am I tired I think I'll try to get to bed early tonight and she finally took the hint and said *well I better be getting on home.* So I didn't dare say oh don't leave so soon like I usually do I just said okay bye.

As soon as she left I turned on the TV and mopped the kitchen floor and then vacuumed the living room rug and then straightened the pillows on the sofa and found a bra and almost threw up. It was not mine. At first I picked it up and looked at it closely because I thought calm down maybe it's been there so long you forgot you had it but it wasn't mine it was too big so then I dropped it back on the sofa but I didn't want it on the sofa so I wiped it onto the floor and then I couldn't think of what to do so I just stared at it for a while like you stare at somebody who's been in a car wreck and then I thought about AIDS and VD and got a piece of paper and picked it up and threw it in the trash can and washed my hands in hot water.

At first I couldn't think of where it came from but then I remembered Rusty and Claire and I thought they have gone too far they just ought to have more respect than to bring girls up here.

If a person were thinking about divorce which I'm not I wonder how many nights the husband would have to be gone for the person to be considered left.

It seems like no matter how sleazy you were you wouldn't forget your own bra.

chapter 6

I decided to help with the bazaar because I missed some LIFE meetings when my eye looked so bad because I hate everybody asking what happened so I told Malone's mother I had to work late even though I knew she would say that's just not right what if you had children and people start to wondering if you're out of fellowship and they already think I'm a little suspect because Malone almost never goes to church and I try to explain that he needs his sleep on Sundays because of dental school but I can tell they think that's no excuse. Sometimes I think they have seen him at a bar but they would have had to go there to do that so maybe I'm just being paranoid. So I'm going to embroider some squares for a quilt they're going to auction off as soon as my finger gets better which it almost is already. And the day before the bazaar I'll bake two cakes for the cakewalk which is enough to get my name in the bulletin and shut everybody up. For a while.

When I'm a lawyer it won't matter if I only go once a month because some people will think if you're a true Christian and a woman you don't have a career but if you have to work you can be a teacher or a secretary or a nurse so I won't be a Christian to them and I don't care and others think if you are a doctor or a lawyer and you go to church at all you are a godly person.

I bet Mr. Jackson goes to church. When I become a lawyer I will find out where he goes and I will go there.

He is back in town but he was very busy yesterday and today catching up on other clients so I didn't say anything to him about Ann Barton and I told Malone and later his mother that he is still out of town because the deal he is working on didn't go through. He said *what do you mean go through*. I said I don't really know but that's what his secretary told me which wasn't exactly true but that has happened before with Mr. Brooks and he'll call me and say cancel all my appointments for tomorrow the deal didn't go through and I've got to stay up here another day. He said *damn*. Malone don't get mad he'll do it as soon as he gets back. He said *you are absolutely worthless as a wife* and I couldn't help it I started crying because what if Mama is right and he was in debt Malone will never forgive me. He said *don't do this to me* and I fell down and said leave me alone and he walked out and slammed the door and I listened to him walk down the hall and I got up and locked the door and got myself some ice and I wanted a glass of wine to help my food digest which the Bible says is okay but we didn't have any so I found some vodka which must have been Claire's or Rusty's because we would never buy it which tasted like medicine but I had a teeny bit anyway because it was basically for medicinal purposes and asked God to forgive me for saying that about the deal.

I lay there watching TV on the couch for a while and then Malone's mother called and said *how's everything*. I said fine. She said *where's Malone*. I said out studying. She said *I figured because he didn't call me today*. I said well he's pretty busy lately. She said *I'm feeling awful lonesome and I imagine you are too so I'll just come on over and you can tell me all about what your Mr. Jackson said*. And I was glad she had called because she doesn't usually she just shows up and I didn't want her to see me so I said well there's nothing to tell he's still out of town so why don't you come over tomorrow instead and I promise I'll have some news because if I didn't say that she would have come over tonight anyway and I might need her tomorrow night although probably not. She said *okay if you don't want me to come tonight*. I said it's not that to tell you the truth I'm not feeling very well tonight. She said *do you think you're pregnant*. I said no. She said *is it serious*. I said no. **49** She said *well maybe you should think about getting pregnant*. I said okay I will. Which I won't although I have forgotten my pills lately but it doesn't matter because we are not doing anything anyway because of finals. She said *good for you now what time should I come tomorrow and what do you want me to bring*. I said any time after six because I don't get home until then and don't bring anything.

So I will have to talk to Mr. Jackson tomorrow.

chapter 7

(Fill in when I get details straight.)

chapter 8

Whatever it is it is horrible.

I may have had a nervous breakdown.

The first thing I remember is lying there and my brain saying you are about to die about to die about to die die die and I opened my eyes I was facing a blank wall with a crack in the paint and the crack got big then small then big then small each time bigger then smaller. Then closing my eyes lights flashing inside my eyelids don't panic don't panic about to die. Hearing heavy breathing breathing heavy no oxygen don't panic.

Don't panic you have a name what is it think of your name think of writing your name on a piece of paper what would you write if this is the first stage of mental illness they will put you in an institution in Iowa so think. I don't know where I am I'm going to die okay look around ground yourself in reality.

The sheets are yellow. You are in a single bed with yellow sheets. You are wearing a pink nightgown. You have on a gold wedding ring. You are right here in a single bed with yellow sheets wearing a pink nightgown where is here. Concentrate on being here and alive. Don't panic you are not going to die. Slow down your breathing don't panic. Focus breathe slowly relax. You are not going to die.

Then I knew. I knew who I was and where I was and I put my finger up to the crack and there was wall behind it. Solid wall. I traced the crack with my finger until it went past the bed and then I traced a fold in the sheet. A clean yellow sheet. A very happy clean yellow sheet.

Until the fold came to me and to keep following it I had to roll over and boom flashing lights again. How did I get here what has happened to make me feel so bad have I been in a car crash is Malone dead did I try to kill myself and fail. I can't think I need help.

Mama. And she said *shh* and wiped off my tears with a Kleenex and stroked my forehead and then she said *would you like some aspirin* and I said yes and she gave me two Tylenol and a glass of water. *How about some tea and toast.* Which thinking about made me feel nauseous. *Okay why don't you get some rest.* What happened. *Just go back to sleep.* My head. *It will feel better soon.* Malone. *Don't worry about him.* Work. *I called and told them you weren't feeling well and would be out for a few days and they said that's fine.* What happened. *Shh don't worry* so I felt worried for a while only I couldn't think of what to worry about and ended up feeling dizzy and going back to sleep. Shh don't worry. Don't panic.

Now I have spent the last two days in bed and it turns out I had a hangover which I promise I will never do again I will repent but it is gone now only I still have bruises on my inside thighs and my wrists and a scraped knee which I don't know where they came from. And I still have an upset stomach. Which all is what I deserve.

I have been trying to remember what happened because Mama says *I don't know all I know is that you showed up on my doorstep in awful shape at 2:30 in the morning and I took you in and put you to bed.* And I still don't remember everything but what I do remember tells me I better get the rest of my tapes and my notebook out of the kitchen drawer why didn't I leave everything in the car. Because if he or his mother finds out what I said about them they will never forgive me or he might even try to kill me. I don't mean kill he would never do such a thing I just mean hate I don't know what I mean. But I don't know how to get them because classes are over for the semester so he and the two of them are liable to be there any time of the day or night plus which I don't feel good enough. **53**

When I think about it I start breathing like when I didn't know who I was.

So I am going to have to make Mama swear on a Bible that she will be careful and she will get them and not read or listen to a word of it and I will tell her you sit outside the building in your car with the doors locked and you wait until he has left the building and if he comes up to you you just start the car and drive away fast but if he leaves then you go up to the apartment and knock on the door and if anyone answers the door make up an excuse and leave fast but if you knock real loud several times and no one comes then let yourself in and run into the kitchen and get the blue notebook and the box of tapes out from under the dishtowels in the bottom drawer by the refrigerator and then run back out and go straight to your car and come home and do not read any of it.

Then I will be safe.

chapter 9

I remember. I woke up in the middle of the night sweating and throbbing all over and I knew.

But I will not write it.

I don't have to write anything I don't want to. I don't have to think about anything I don't want to or anybody.

I may never write again.

I may kill myself.

I may kill Malone.

I might call the police I might I don't know what I will do.

chapter 10

This is what happened. If anyone reads this you will know why I did what I did. It is all true. It is the truth, the whole truth, and nothing but the truth.

Tuesday morning everything was normal. I got to work early and I filled out all my message sheets for Mr. Ballard and Mr. Brooks and then I filled out one for Mr. Jackson. It said my mother's attorney's name is Ann Barton she works for Smith, Habeth and Fornam thank you very much for offering to help and I signed it. And then I pretended I was him and read it and said yuck so I wrote another one. It said Ann Barton on one line and Smith, Habeth and Fornam on the next and I figured I would say the rest because I didn't want anyone to see anything on his desk about him helping me. So I tore the first one in half and then in half again and again and again and then I looked at each piece and no piece had more than two letters on it and wadded them up into little paper balls and threw them away. Which was good. That was the first memo sheet I have torn but I did it on purpose so I don't think it counts. I have seventy-nine message sheets at home and I have still never torn one when I was pulling it off the pad.

And then I got the good one and walked down to his office and practiced on the way. Hi Mr. Jackson I have the name of my mother's attorney that you asked for last week. And he would say oh thanks I'll get right on that. Thanks I really appreciate your help. And he would say why don't I tell you what I find out over lunch. Oh okay that sounds nice. I'll come by your desk about 12:00 and he would touch me on the arm. Which there would be nothing wrong with because we are just friends and business associates and with me being married and all he wouldn't push for more than that no matter how he felt and I would never think of anything more. If you leave your husband for another man you can't get married again or you will be committing adultery. Only if he leaves you.

But he wasn't there yet, although his secretary, Camille, was right across the hall. She must know that I will be friends with Mr. Jackson because I am going to law school, because she is already jealous of me. His door was open so I looked in but his light wasn't on and she said *what do you want*. And I said I have a message for Mr. Jackson. And she said *what is it* because she acts possessive of him like she thinks she's his wife. And I smiled and said it's personal I'll just tell him later. And she was so jealous she couldn't think of anything to say so she just started typing but I bet at her first break she told everybody. I don't care because I don't care what non-Christians think about me. For example if they reject me then I am in good company because they have also rejected Christ and there is a special blessing in Heaven for those who have been persecuted for His name's sake.

So I went back to my desk and put the good one in my purse and started filing a stack of papers for Mr. Ballard but then I started thinking about Mr. Jackson and how I had to talk to him today but what if I don't get the chance or if somebody else hears us or he forgot and I tell him Ann Barton and he says what about her. And I got a horrible headache and it was only 9:00 which means that I would have to be there for eight more hours because even if I come in early I stay until five because whatsoever your hand finds to do do it heartily as unto the Lord and also if I went home early some of his friends might be there fornicating with that bra. They know I get off at five.

Then I got the good one out of my purse and looked up the phone number for Smith, Habeth and Fornam and wrote it down on the message sheet under Smith, Habeth and Fornam and the whole message looked more centered with it there. Then I put it back in my purse and told myself quit thinking about it because you can think things to death if you're not careful and work until 10:30 and then go down there and do it because you have to. And I figured that an hour and a half was long enough to wait so as not to look too eager to Camille. So at 10:30 I just got the good one out of my purse and stood up and said go and went and he was there and his door was open but so was she right across the hall where she could hear everything we said unless I closed the door which I didn't want to do because that would make the whole thing seem too formal or sneaky. So I stood there in the doorway and said very casually knock knock. And he looked up and said *hi*. And I said I have that name you were asking me for and hesitated just one second to see if he knew what I meant because I didn't want Camille to hear him say what name but I didn't want her to hear me say my mother's lawyer either so he looked like he almost knew so I said a little quieter the lawyer. And he said *oh yeah*. And I thought whew and walked over to his desk and put it down on the edge and didn't say anything because I forgot the name but I knew enough to know how stupid it would look to read my own message to him right there in

57

front of him. He picked it up and looked at it and said *Ann Barton I can't believe this I went to law school with Ann* only the way he said it you would have thought he went to bed with her so I started walking back toward the door and said it's a small world or something idiotic like that. And he said *I'll get on this right away.* And I said thanks.

About 2:00 he comes over to my desk and says *I talked to Ann.* But Angie was five feet away and I didn't want her to hear how rich I am and I couldn't believe he would be so insensitive as to not think of that so I said well I've got to finish this letter by 2:30 but why don't I come to your office and hear all about her then. He said *fine see you* and walks down the hall and I knew something was up from the way he was carrying himself and my headache practically went away and what was left was just excitement. Angie said *who's Ann.* And I thought none of your beeswax and said just a mutual friend.

And I waited until 2:25 and said long enough and went down there and Camille wasn't at her desk so I went in his office and closed the door very casually almost like it closed itself and said what's the scoop and I wasn't even nervous because he seemed so positive like he had great news and I didn't mind if he knew how rich I was and he didn't know I would have to use it to pay off Malone's debt he would just think I was rich. But he said *what has your mother told you.* And I thought this is strange and my headache came back a little and I sat down in his chair for clients and said well let's see not too much um just that she won't give me any money basically. And he said *did she tell you that your father had some pretty bad setbacks and owed a lot of money.* I said she mentioned something like that but my or I figured it out she's just saying that because of grief she has turned into a greedy person you know from grief and everything and then I decided I was saying too much so I quit. He took a deep breath and my head got worse and he said very slowly and quietly *I'll put it to you straight the truth is that he had borrowed against the business the house and his life insurance policy which of course wouldn't have paid anyway but things don't look good for your mother.* And I thought don't get emotional and said very calmly that is not true did you talk to her. And he said *no I had lunch with Ann and she had received your mother's permission to show me the bank's papers and the insurance company's papers and the will and everything there was to see there's no question about it so I really think you ought to just drop the whole thing and get on with your life.* And I couldn't believe how my mother had brainwashed her lawyer and her lawyer had brainwashed Mr. Jackson so I couldn't say anything I just sat there looking at the edge of the desk. He said *hey I'm sorry if I can do anything.* And I thought what are you going to do and I said no I'm fine and I couldn't look at him and I couldn't get up and walk out because Camille would be at her desk and I couldn't think of what to do and he said *would you like a Coke* and I shook my head yes and he went out and closed the door behind him.   59

By the time he came back I had drawn on those wells of strength which I may do again now and I may not because what's the point and he was impressed with how calm I was and even smiling which I thought his mother (M's) would say was a witness to him (Mr. Jackson) of the grace of God but it turns out she wouldn't have meant it but which I know was because I am a very strong person and I will do fine in law school and I won't need that money or even Mr. Jackson because I will find someone better. For a friend and business associate. Or either they will all be sorry because I will be so beautiful they will not be able to do anything else and it will remind them all of how helpless they are without me.

Both my grandmothers were fat and got diabetes in their old age because of it. Which is a horrible disease and I will never get fat no matter what so I won't get it. But I have ruled out anorexia nervosa too because it is too slow and even though you look great at first by the end which is your last impression you look gross. I have also ruled out asphyxiation by a plastic bag or a pillow because the pillow would be too hard and the bag ruins the whole effect when you are found. But not by gas. Also no drowning or being left outside during the summer I just found out you can swell up so much your clothes rip off. I'm never going to watch the Incredible Hulk the same way again. I wonder if you can get a sunburn after you're dead. The thing is to have your body outside during a long cold dry spell so no matter how long it takes them to find you you won't be rotten. Which rules out gas.

So that night I got home about 5:30 and thought I would lie down and think up a plan but she was already there and when I walked in the door she runs out of the kitchen and hugs me and says *oh I'm so glad you're home* and I try to smile because I'm not ready for her to know but she guesses that something is wrong and says *don't tell me he's still out of town*. I should have said yes. Or no but now Mama's lawyer is out of town. Or he decided not to help. But I said it's not that. And she said *well what's wrong*. And I said why don't we wait till he gets home I don't want to have to explain this twice but then I thought maybe it would be better if she already knew and she could help calm him down instead of being as shocked as he will be. So I said never mind I'll tell you the truth is that he had borrowed against the business the house and the life insurance so Mama didn't even get that and she really didn't inherit any-thing but debt and all of the sudden my head was worse than ever and I had to sit down and I wanted to kick his mother for what she had made me do to my mama. And she said *Damn* which I was sure at the time was her first time ever.

And I keep seeing her face saying *Damn. Damn. Damn. Damn.*

So when he got home somehow we told him and he didn't even stay for dinner he just got mad and left and she left after him so I was all alone and the ambulances outside were going crazy and I thought what am I going to do now. And I locked the door and got a bottle of vodka which was a sin I don't know why I did it temporary insanity from stress no I take full responsibility for it and claim the Lord's forgiveness and took the TV into the bedroom and locked the bedroom door and went to bed.

And everything I forgot I wish I still forgot it but I don't have to go through it again now.

Sometimes I try to remember more details but it feels too strange so I think the Lord must not want me to know so maybe I shouldn't try anymore and sometimes I try to forget what I do remember but I can't help it my mind just goes there and it plays itself over in my mind like a broken record.

My mother feels sorry for me but also like I deserve this for what I did to her. And nobody else cares at all.

I am not going to do it right now because I don't know the best way plus which it is not cold enough outside. Also because I sort of don't want to. I don't know why. Maybe I am not finished yet. Maybe I am a coward.

chapter 10

This is really chapter sixteen. It turns out we didn't start over after all. It almost feels like Chapter 1 because I feel sort of like a new person I view the world differently now. But I am not going to participate in the ridiculous fiction of naming this time in my life Chapter 1 it doesn't work. This is not the beginning. A beginning maybe. There is no such thing as the beginning beginning is a time before which there is nothing and you always have something that comes before. Even God is eternal there never was nothing. Yes in the beginning God in the beginning the Word but that is in the beginning of time and God existed before time. So I will start a new chapter but not a new beginning. Now every chapter will be numbered not because they have some divine order to them but because that is how life works we exist within the constraints of time one day comes after the next and even if you feel like you're a different person on the seventeenth than you were on the sixteenth you don't start the calendar over and even if you don't feel like a new person on January first which most people don't you can't call it December thirty-second. Sometimes you want to start over and you can't and sometimes you don't want to but you have to.

Plus it doesn't matter because I will rewrite and re-number everything for my autobiography anyway.

chapter 16

I will have to reorganize all my tapes and notes I can't remember what goes where and I was trying to keep track by starting off writing or saying chapter something every time but now it's all messed up I don't know if I'll ever get it straightened out. My tapes and my notebook came back plus some panties and clothes so I am happy well I am content I have everything I need. I am going to use these notes to write an autobiography which will illustrate the strength of modern woman against tribulation and the loss of God in modern society and be a best seller and I will go on *Oprah Winfrey* and be rich and famous and everybody will know what he did to me and they will say that is one amazing woman do you know what he did to her.

I will have to add my childhood which won't be hard because it was uneventful. I was born in St. Vincent's hospital in Birmingham and my parents lived in a two-bedroom apartment on Southside which was a fairly nice area at the time. I don't remember this so I will just mention it in the first chapter and then move on. I will not tell about Uncle Dwight because all that is nobody's business.

My first memory is in this house in this room. I was three or four, maybe five, but five seems a little old for a first memory and people might think I was stupid so three. I had a gold dress with black plaid stripes that buttoned down the front with black buttons and white cuffs and collar and a black bow at the neck which my mother wanted me to wear but I knew it looked like a boy's shirt and that she wanted me to be a boy and I tried to kiss my elbow which if you did you would turn into a boy but I couldn't.

65

Another one is my first kindergarten which I hated because you had to go up and down these stairs all the time and the fat teacher always stood on the top stair and you had to squeeze by her but she did it because that stair was loose and if she didn't we would all fall down. I still hate it when men stand right in the doorway and motion for ladies to go through first but the only way you can is to squeeze past them.

Then I changed kindergartens because my mother said when the carpool came to pick me up for the first kindergarten I would scream and kick and she would have to carry me out and dump me in the car although I don't necessarily remember that I've just heard about it so many times like Uncle Dwight says about the time he was six and they went to Disneyland and he rode the teacup ride and then threw up on Mickey Mouse right when he was having his picture made I don't remember it but I'll never forget it so she found another one and my father came in this room to tuck me in this bed and said why don't we pray that God will provide a friend for you in your new kindergarten which we did and He did, Lalie Martin (pronounced Lollie. Her real name was Eulalia Antoinette Martin, which I thought was the most beautiful name in the world. We called her Lollie-Pop.) and we stayed best friends until sixth grade when Anna Mary Lambert stole her.

My father always took me to church and Mother decided she didn't have to go because she was good enough already but I have never been good enough even though if she is good enough you don't have to be that good and the Sunday school teacher said *you are lost but you can be found you are broken but you can be made whole don't you want to be saved by being baptized into a true relationship with the father.* And I did if somebody can save me I want to be saved and I loved my daddy I really did and I wish I could tell him now because I didn't act like it for a while. So we went after church to talk to the preacher and I thought I must be sick or dying because they were going to have to wash me in lamb's blood although later they changed their minds about that part but he looked at my face for a long time and said *you are a very special child to me* and I thought do you mean as in retarded because he made me feel strange and he said he will put me under water and say some things and my spirit will die and experience new birth and enter a new relationship with your father and it won't hurt so don't be afraid but fortunately I had heard that before at the doctor's office so when they put me under I held my breath just in case. And then it was over nothing had happened I was still lost and broken or whatever I was before but they all thought it had and I had fooled them and my father was so happy that I had done it that I almost wished it was true and I had died.

chapter 17

My father was a lot like Mr. Jackson. Very gentle and compassionate. Tall with broad shoulders. I went back to work
today although I am still staying with my mother so I don't
have to cook and things besides which finals are over and
when she went to get my stuff she said most of his clothes
were gone so he must have gone on a trip. Which I say
good riddance I hope he stays gone. It's just that we can't
afford it and I haven't even had a chance to find out about
the insurance and since I quit wearing my splint he probably
forgot about it but I still have to pay the bill and it's just
not right of him to spend that kind of money on a trip. I
know he is head of the house and I said at our wedding I

would obey him and I do that was a solemn oath to God and I take that seriously never go back on an oath you make to God that is serious business. But it seems to me there ought to be limits that there are still certain things that belong to me that there ought to be some money for example that I could say that's mine I earned it and if you take it on a trip and spend it all on yourself without even asking me you're stealing and there ought to be certain times when I could say no and he would have to stop that he could order me to submit but I could say no it's still my body that I could say no about the things that are mine and I wouldn't be breaking my oath to God. Malone says *no you said love honor and obey* he says obey real loud *you didn't say obey when you feel like it* but I still say there's a problem.

Stop. I will control my thoughts. I will not think about that.

When Mr. Jackson got in he made a special trip over to my desk and he said *are you okay*. And I looked right into his eyes and he looked into mine and I barely shook my head no and said just a little bug and we understood each other. Nobody noticed the bruises because being almost Christmas it is very natural to wear long sleeves even though we are having a warm spell. They are healing very quickly. I have great recuperative powers.

Mother had made me a lunch and by coincidence I happened to go into the kitchen to eat it a few minutes after he had brought in a salad from the sandwich shop downstairs because being a bachelor he never brings his own lunch even when he doesn't want to go out. And he was reading a book so I said what are you reading. And he said *Mrs. Dalloway*. And I had heard of that and I said who was it that wrote that. *Virginia Wolfe*. Oh yeah I love her. He said *I like her too* and I thought about saying something like who's afraid of Virginia Wolfe but I have just heard that phrase I don't know what it means or maybe it's just a joke about the big bad wolf because she was a mean person so I am going to have to go to the library tomorrow during lunch and read something about her so I will have been telling the truth but meanwhile I thought I better change the subject but for some reason he makes me nervous not like the preacher used to but still. So I was just finished with half of my sandwich but I said well I better get back to work bye. And he watched me as I walked out of the room.

My mother had the preacher and his wife over for dinner tonight which was horrible. She isn't even religious much less a born-again Christian so I don't know why she did it. Yes I do. She probably told him my daughter's going nuts so why don't you come over and observe and tell me what to do because preachers are free and psychiatrists cost a lot of money.

Which reminds me. It is too late tonight but tomorrow I will call Mrs. Butler who is in charge of the bazaar and say I am staying with my mother who is very sick and depressed and needs me to take care of her so I won't be **69** able to help with the bazaar and also I will take her to her own church until she gets better so she will tell our LIFE group to pray for her and they will know why I'm not there and maybe Malone's mother will hear and feel sorry for me. I don't know what Malone has told her but she hasn't called which makes me think he told her I did something horrible. Which I did.

Malone you I can't even say it. You make me so mad I can hardly write. I hope God heaps burning coals on your head.

chapter 15
I think

She spelled her last name Woolf I thought it was Wolfe and
she wasn't mean so I still don't know about who's afraid of
Virginia Woolf or maybe I just made that up. She killed
herself by putting rocks in her pockets and walking out into
a river and they didn't find her body until three weeks later
and I'm sure it was all distorted and they had it cremated
which I haven't even thought of burial or cremation but it
seems like drowning was a bad idea although it might have
been appropriate because she wrote a book called *The Waves*
which was at the library but I didn't check it out because I
read the first page and it was too boring but maybe if you
read it you would think drowning fit with her personality

because I think you should do it in a way that expresses something about you. For example Ernest Hemingway was very macho and he killed himself by shooting himself in the head which is very powerful like he was hunting and it takes a strong act of will to pull the trigger when it's pointed at you when I couldn't even pull one on a squirrel not because I believe in animal rights because we were sent here to dominate the earth but because it would be too gross whereas drowning involves more of a release of will in that you have to stop trying and let yourself die. Passive v. Active. I would not drown myself because it would remind people of my father. And I would never shoot myself or anyone else.

They had *Mrs. Dalloway* in the card catalogue but not in the shelves like it was checked out so it must be a popular book but I just looked through whatever they had where *Mrs. Dalloway* was supposed to be and got a book about her 71 that I thought might summarize *Mrs. Dalloway*. It didn't. Libraries do not have Cliff Notes. I had forgotten that. College bookstores do I should have gone to the UAB bookstore but at least this was free.

She was bisexual. I don't understand how because it seems like she loved her husband. But I know it is very wrong. Worse than fornication. And grosser if you think about it. This was before AIDS but I think God created AIDS because of people like that. Bi sounds worse than homo. I don't know why Mr. Jackson would read an author like that. Maybe you can't tell from *Mrs. Dalloway* and he doesn't know.

I don't know why I haven't thought about being buried or cremated. I know I don't want to be cremated because I don't want my body not to exist anymore or to be spread over a forest but I don't want to keep it in an urn because who will take care of it in a hundred years. Or even right after I die. One of the lawyers at work said the other day that his wife bought an antique silver piece at a flea market because she thought it was pretty and she put it on a mantel and you guessed it it turned out to be somebody's ashes because a guest recognized what it was but nobody knew whose they were and everybody got a big laugh out of it but that could have been me so I will never be cremated. But if you think about being buried it feels claustrophobic at first and then look at your arm and think about the skin rotting off and being eaten by bugs while you're just lying there not even moving. In which case cremation doesn't seem so bad.

I have thought about a suicide note but not exactly what I would say. One thing. It will not be addressed to anyone in particular and I wish it would be so good that it would be printed in the newspapers. Virginia Woolf's was great. I have read it twenty times. She wrote it to her (male) husband:

> Dearest,
> I feel certain that I am going mad again: I feel we cant go through another of those terrible times. And I shant recover this time. I begin to hear voices, and cant concentrate. So I am going to do what seems the best thing to do. You have given me the greatest possible happiness. You have been in every way all that anyone could be. I dont think two people could have been happier till this terrible disease came. I cant fight it any longer, I know that I am spoiling your life, that without me you could work. And you will I know. You see I cant even write this properly. I cant read. What I want to say is that I owe all the happiness of my life to you. You have been entirely patient with me and incredibly good. I want to say that—everybody knows it. If anybody could have saved me it would have been you. Everything has gone from me but the certainty of your goodness. I cant go on spoiling your life any longer.
> I dont think two people could have been happier than we have been.
> V.

If somebody that good loved me I wouldn't do it. Maybe by the end she was normal again in terms of sex. Think about not thinking two people could have been happier than you have been. I have been wondering if other people were as miserable as me. No I haven't I am handling this remarkably well I am very strong I draw on the wells of the strength of God. The Bible teaches that the unrighteous will sometimes profit but it won't last. Which must be why she had to kill herself. God made her.

I wonder why she didn't use apostrophes and how she could be a famous writer if she didn't know basic grammar. What is this world coming to.

My book will have all the apostrophes it needs. Whatsoever your hand finds to do do it heartily as unto the Lord.

I keep thinking I'll hear from Malone. I don't know where he is or if he is okay and sometimes when I think about him I feel so mad I can't stand it and sometimes I burst into tears including once at the office. So I put him **73** out of my mind be strong and go on. If God is giving me this situation He must know that I can handle it He is right.

I hope he comes home for Christmas not because I think everything would be perfect just that we could be okay for one day and maybe that would lead to one more day and one more day and we could rebuild. And even if not pretending would be better than being alone on Christmas. I can be forgiving and I want to have a Christian marriage if he never comes back I will be a reject a failure. I bought him a real nice green wool sweater. I think it is wrong to feel sorry for yourself about a situation that is your own fault so I will not. But if he has left me I want to point out that he is more wrong. Because it wasn't entirely my fault I was drunk and I have admitted that but he was worse than that and I said no and husband or no husband you don't do it when the other person says no when I said love honor and obey I'm not sure exactly what I meant but I know what I didn't mean I didn't mean that.

I bought his mother and my mother each a cookbook. I think it is funny to have only three people in the world to buy Christmas presents for. I always thought when I got married and got a job things would be different.

I think I have made a mistake.

I just thought of something. You could have your ashes put in an airtight container and be buried with a marker and everything. On second thought that's not such a good idea because it sounds like a Tupperware grave and even more claustrophobic than a coffin. And if it leaked you would turn into mud.

chapter 16

Christmas wasn't too bad. Of course he wasn't here but I don't care. I had an upset stomach but we slept late which was good because I have been very tired lately what with the stress of him being gone and everything and Mother made a turkey and invited the preacher and his wife over for lunch (again) so they entertained her and I didn't have to say anything and nobody noticed that I wasn't eating much and when they left she had a lot of cleaning up to do and I put on my new dress and fixed my hair and went over to the apartment but he wasn't back yet or maybe he was at his mother's who still hasn't called me and I thought about going over there to give her the cookbook but for some reason I feel strange about that. I feel strange about most things lately. So I got the mail out of the mailbox and took what was mine and the bills including a second notice on the medical bills and left his on the counter and watched TV for a while in case he came back I don't know what I expected I guess I just wanted to see him and say hi and then I went to the bathroom and sat on the toilet and stared at the seam in the wallpaper which was not put up right because it is plaid and the stripes don't come together on each side of the seam they are about a fourth of an inch apart and sometimes I hate it so much I have to close my eyes when I use the bathroom but then it was getting dark and it started raining and the apartment started depressing me so I got some books to read and left. I had planned to get some more clothes but I couldn't go in the bedroom.

If I were Mr. Jackson's secretary I would buy him Virginia Woolf's biography which would show how well read I am and also how well I know him. Also I think he ought to know about her. I wonder what he would buy me.

So much could be different. So much changed this year. I wonder what will happen next year.

I better stop now. I feel sad.

chapter 17

Mr. Jackson went to Georgia for Christmas but he is back now. I went to work today and I am glad Christmas is over and everything is back to normal. There.

And things are pretty much back to normal with his mother. I think I have been through the worst part of a crisis and am coming out of it just fine. It's those wells of strength. Now I know what weathering a storm really means. She called me at work and said *how've you been*. And my hands went cold and I said oh great how about you. She said *pretty good*. Good. *How was your Christmas.* Good. *Well I'd love to hear all about it and tell you all about mine so why don't you come over here for dinner tonight.* And I felt like I couldn't remember who

I was even though I remembered who I was I don't know
why but then I thought maybe he's back and he contacted
her first because he was afraid I am mad which I'm not he
can take a lot from me but he can't take my faith anger is
a poison to the faith so I am using this situation to build
patience long-suffering although Mama is mad as Hell (her
words not mine) and says he is trash and you ought to dump
him but she doesn't have a husband now so she doesn't want
me to have one can you believe a grown woman would
begrudge her own daughter a chance for success well she
would so I know it's not polite but my mouth said who's
going to be there. And she said *just the two of us*. And I thought
too bad or okay or good I really couldn't figure out what to
think and then I thought of the cookbook and I said I have
a Christmas present for you and only after I said that did I
think that will give her time to buy me one if she hasn't
already. And she said *oh you shouldn't have done that* and I
thought why not I'm your son's wife aren't I and she said
but I have one for you too and I couldn't tell if she was making
it up or not.

So I went home (to Mother's) after work and got the
cookbook and brushed my hair and put on fresh makeup
on top of what I wore to work and went over to her house.
I don't know if my brain is working exactly right because I
can't remember driving over there. I know what streets you
have to take so I figure I took them but I can't remember
actually taking them tonight. Like I was mechanical.

And we ate pot roast with carrots and potatoes and
homemade biscuits which is my favorite and she said *well if
this wasn't the strangest Christmas ever I don't know what was.* And
I just looked at her and picked up a biscuit and said yeah.
And she said *I mean one minute I'm making up my grocery list for
Christmas dinner and next thing I know I'm packing to go to Macon.*
Me buttering my biscuit and going yeah that's weird thinking
what in the heck are you talking about. *Well I don't know how
much Malone has told you but you'll be glad to know that Mitzie I
don't think you've ever met her she's my Aunt Caroline's youngest girl*

and she went into labor even though she was only six months pregnant and lost the baby bless her heart and almost died herself but you'll be glad to know that she made it through all right and now she's pretty much back to normal. What happened. *You never know do you but I think it was the grace of God giving Mitzie a chance to straighten herself out.* Probably. *I mean she's always been one to sow her wild oats pretty freely if you know what I mean but when she got pregnant well you can imagine what everybody said and poor Caroline just bore it all like a saint.* Yeah, finishing my biscuit. *And I always say the Lord will never give you more than you can bear.* That's true. Silence. *Well anyway how about you how was your Christmas.* Fine nice. *And is Malone having fun in Pensacola* like she thought I already knew so I acted like I did even though I thought can't you see anything and I said oh I guess so. And she said *his friend's father's condo sure sounds nice doesn't it.* Sure does. *I let that money I sent him when you couldn't get off work in time to get to Western Union count for his Christmas present from me but I have a little something here for you* and she got up to get it which was a relief because I haven't gotten a bank statement yet but I was afraid he had taken all of ours when he left so I have only spent Mama's not mine and just not paid the big bills like the doctor bill but maybe I will take out what I would have spent and open an account that he doesn't know about only in my name just in case would that be like stealing who cares. And I forgot about acting he makes me so furious sometimes but I couldn't explain and when she came back in the room she said *cheer up I'm sure he misses you and if you could have gotten off work he would have taken you.* And I thought cheer up this is great advice and I said oh yeah he told me that. And she said *here* and gave me a box and I opened it and it was a wreath of grape vine and dried flowers and I said this is beautiful I love it which was true I do it is probably worth twenty or thirty dollars and then she said *Caroline made it herself can you believe that.* Wow. And then it was quiet for a minute. She said *when do classes start up again.* I said a week or two I'm not sure. *Don't you know what day he's coming home.* Well I have it written down but. *Isn't he coming home the day*

79

before classes start. I thought so but now he talks like he might come home earlier. *Oh.* She can be incredibly stupid.

This is what I got for Christmas:

Object:	From:
Dress	Mother
Wreath	His Mother
(TBA)	Him

I am sure that he will give me something when he gets back he is probably buying something down there. But if he doesn't I will wear the sweater I bought him with jeans so either way I get something.

I am already thinking of my New Year's resolutions because so many strange things happened this year that won't happen next year and everything will be better. Or if it's not then this will be my last year. One will be be a better Christian because I have not really read the Bible every night even though I said I did. One will be be a better wife not that I have been unfaithful but it's up to the wife to create an environment in the home that will make the husband happy there although realistically what else can I do think of something. One will be make more money. One will be stop having bad dreams because they are getting worse. I will have ten altogether but I haven't thought of all of them. Because Malone and I got off to a bad start and formed some bad habits but now things will change and as soon as he gets back he will call me and I will tell him all this and I will say it was good that you went away because it gave us both some time to think and he will say that's why I went because I care so much. Or either he will say I don't care about you anymore I have to face that possibility and then I will have to win him without a word by my behavior. Or we will go our separate ways I can't go away from him I can't imagine life without him I need him and he needs me. Everybody says your first year of marriage is a big adjustment so just stick it out and then you will be fine. Plus all things work together for good and if you are a Christian you ought to experience the joy of the Lord all the time. Another will be experience the joy of the Lord all the time. Another will be be healthier because lately I don't feel so good. I am all confused.

I am trying as hard as I can. I am really trying to be a good person to do what's right. I mean I'm practically sweating right now I'm trying so hard. I'm just trying to be optimistic not to lose faith because when you lose your faith you've lost everything. I'm really trying to glorify God to live a Christian life this is what I was put on this earth to do it's important.

But sometimes it's very hard.

I think Satan is trying to discourage me there is a spiritual battle taking place in my soul and I will not let him win.

chapter 18

It is New Year's Eve and I am home alone because Mama
is at a party but I am not because I was not invited to one.
So I ate Lean Cuisine zucchini lasagna and fudge ripple ice
cream that is basically vanilla they never put enough fudge
for dinner and I am watching TV with no sound while I
tape this and I am still eating the ice cream out of the carton
which is on a plate so it won't drip even though Mother's
couch is so yucky that a little fudge ripple spilled all over
it would be an improvement and Dick Clark just came on.
I can't stand him. I wish he would grow up. Not having
sound makes you realize how stupid they all are. I try to
have fudge in every bite so I am down to the bottom of the

box in some places and still on the top in others. And all those people in New York think they're the center of the universe so they all hug each other. Smile for the camera. Smiling is not the joy of the Lord which I will have every day of the year starting tomorrow. I think New Year's Eve is the stupidest holiday of the year. It makes me want to cuss. Damn. Shit. Damn. I hate TV commercials. Especially when they have children who think they are cute in them. Children who think they are cute are just about the most disgusting variety of human beings alive. Gays are first. They are second. Gays are first because they are even disgusting to God and He made them. God likes children because they are easier for Him to manipulate than adults. He didn't make them gay He just made them.

What if it is all over what if he were not coming back what would it feel like.

83

It isn't over because I would feel it I would know and I don't feel anything.

I feel like a failure I am fallen I am depraved. I have sinned I am in a failed marriage. I have sinned I deserve the wages of sin.

I just can't do it I don't have the nerve or the equipment what equipment I don't know I haven't decided yet that is another thing but I don't have any equipment and it is too much trouble. Plus think about how much trouble it would be for somebody to make arrangements and nobody would want to and people who just don't care about me would end up hating me because I am so much trouble. Do not think about the future.

I am trying not to think about the past but it thinks for me. What is the passive tense of think I am thought the past is thought the past thinks itself in me.

I know that I am guilty of many sins but they are in the past and they will stay there I do not let myself feel guilt. Guilt is destructive and I must survive. Maybe guilt is a need like love is a need but we can't worry about filling that need until we fill more basic needs. I can think of many horrible things but none of them seem real. When I play back my tapes they don't sound like me talking. That is not what happened. I am a liar on top of everything else. I can't remember what I made up and what I didn't at least not where one stops and the other starts but I know I didn't love him and that we weren't married in the true sense of the word so now even though it would be called divorce that is not what it would be more like annulment or even more like never happened.

I feel a certain strange power. Like I can rewrite the past and start over and certain things will never have happened and certain things will have and I will be beautiful and other people will know it they will say she was very beautiful I will never forget how beautiful she was.

How to accomplish this:

Step 1: Go back into the past the way it is in order to finish that version before you start a new one.

Step 2: Forget the old version. Destroy all evidence of it.

Step 3: Remember the new version. Go through every detail and remember every one. Find evidence for it.

First I will have to pay the medical bills or get Mother to I will get Mother to because he never bought insurance for me. Only for himself. That Bastard. (Sorry.) There is no point in crying over spilled milk. This is what has happened I have to accept it, fix it, and move on to the next version. Fortunately it did not leave a scar. Scars are what makes it hard to rewrite. You can rewrite why you got them into an accident but you cannot wipe them away. This is all garbage you cannot change the past you cannot change anything you can only forget. You can erase the memory of them but they still leave a trace behind.

When you write a word on paper and make a mistake you can only cross it out if you're using a pen but it is still there and you can still read it and crossing it out only calls more attention to it and when you read over it you want to read that part even more and if you're writing in pencil you can erase but you can never completely erase something usually you can still see the ghost of the word and even if you can't X rays could so it's not gone it stays there haunting the page.

The grass withers the flower fades but the word stands forever.

But if you use a word processor you can't cross something out because you don't like it now or you made a mistake and then peek under the cross-out later and say that is what I meant after all because it leaves a glow on the screen for a second but then it is gone forever. At first I hated the word processor at work because all the information was in there but it wasn't anywhere, not in a place that you can touch and say here is that chart in my hand. You can print a copy of the chart but The Chart is still in the computer and you can never touch it and even if it's not a chart if it's a letter or some ideas or something you feel you can't touch it. But now I like it because it is better. My mind is not a blank tablet for people to write on it is a computer it is a dictaphone and I am the operator and I can delete whatever somebody else wrote on it that I don't want to process. Not whatever but some things. Many things. I don't know how the dictaphone stores sounds but if you erase a dictaphone does it leave traces I don't know. The trouble with tapes is that they are all or nothing if you just erase some then you leave a scar of silence which may be worse than what you erased.

I am still afraid of being alone I am not afraid of being alone I am afraid of being alone and being haunted by memories of him. I am not afraid of dying alone I want to die alone. I am afraid of never having children or real love or happiness all that.

What if I couldn't delete everything only erase and everything was still here except not Here. Not mine anymore. And what would I do if I saw him in the store or on the street because he would be a scar. I can't wipe him out.

It would be better if he had died because then people would feel sorry for me and we would have had a wonderful marriage but now I will have been publicly rejected and anybody will not want used goods who could have fresh and I wouldn't want them if they would settle for me because that is probably because they have to and people at church won't understand about what didn't happen and what did and they won't know nobody will know that it is not my fault it is Fate or God's Will or What Happened and I couldn't change it then any more than I can't change it now and God would forgive me but they won't or maybe He wouldn't either because I rebelled and cussed and did many horrible things and maybe this is all a punishment which He thinks I deserve and He doesn't love me anymore. But in a way it is His fault because He should have protected me more and I couldn't handle all that Daddy dying and no money and him pressuring me all the time and not knowing what to do and Mama practically having a nervous break-down not able to help me when I needed it most when I always heard He won't give you anything you can't handle well He did. It was too much. And that is not my fault. It was just too much and I couldn't handle it I am not Superman sometimes I need help and nobody was there.

*

Here are my New Year's resolutions:

1. Experience the joy of the Lord all the time.
2. Be a better wife.
3. Be a better Christian.
4. Be healthier.
5. Don't drink at all.
6. Stop having bad dreams.
7. Be nicer to children.
8. Make more money.
9. Write autobiography.
10. Stop biting fingernails.

Certain people would say that I ought to put stop cussing on there but that is too much for one year.

Under Experience the joy of the Lord all the time I will do this: smile more often. Think of happy things if I get sad. Under Be a better wife I will do this: try a new recipe every week. Under Be a better Christian: read the Bible every night. Under Be healthier: eat more poultry. Under Don't drink at all: don't drink at all. Under Stop having bad dreams: think of nice things while I go to sleep. Maybe I have let the sun go down on my anger once or twice without realizing it. Under Be nicer to children: never get mad when I am in a store and one starts crying. Under Make more money I don't know yet. Under Write auto-biography: record all childhood memories for at least thirty minutes a day. Under Stop biting fingernails: chew gum. I should be a much better person by this time next year. Either way I will not be the same. Maybe I could sell my auto-biography for $100,000.

chapter

Dear heavenly God please please please make this not have
happened please don't punish me or if you have to not this
way please please I don't even know how to ask you but
please please please stop all this from happening please be
merciful for I have sinned and I mean it I am sorry it turned
out this way this isn't what I meant to happen but if you
don't do something I will have lost everything my husband
my mother who is my only family my health my future
everything I can think of that's important and even what's
not important I am losing even my hair. Please. I will put
Stop cussing in place of Stop biting fingernails which will
save money on gum and I want to point out that even when

I cussed I never took your name in vain which is more than I can say for some people who claim to be Christians. And under Be nicer to children I will add visit an orphanage to what is already there I promise I will be a better person but please please if you love me just fix this one thing. I believe I really believe and you said that if we believe and ask then whatever we ask you will do you promised and I promise I really do believe so you will do it because if you didn't keep your promise which I believe you will then you wouldn't be God and you are so I claim the verse that says if you have the faith of a mustard seed then you can say to a mountain move and it will move and I have more faith than that because I have seen a mustard seed it is small and God my faith is big and I believe so I claim your healing power on the situation please heal it like it was never even sick or even stronger. In the name of the Father and the Son and the Holy Spirit in whom I believe. Amen. Praise God from whom all blessings flow. Praise Him all creatures here below. Praise Him above ye heavenly hosts. Praise Father Son and Holy Ghost. Amen.

He is back and I am a total failure and I can't believe this is happening to me because I have been a bad person and rebelled against my mother which is a sin and which I will confess and ask for forgiveness but it is too late God has already punished me. I know because I called the school and I said when do classes start for first-years. And she said *they started yesterday*. And I said so all the first-year students are back from vacation. And she said *as far as I know*. And I thought oh no what has happened so after work I went over there and I didn't knock I just walked in which I realize now a mistake I should have knocked but I didn't and I walked in the living room and nobody was there and then I heard a noise in the bedroom and I looked and they were all three there. Without any clothes on. And all three were big.

What they were doing I don't know none of my business this is disgusting this is not true honorable just pure lovely gracious excellent worthy of praise don't think on these things I shouldn't have even said that.

So I ran back out into the hall and closed the door and I almost wet my pants in fact I did just a teeny bit and then I sat down on the floor because I was having a dizzy spell and he said just a minute basically except that he cussed but I will not repeat what he said I will not even think it. He cussed a lot tonight. And so did I because I had not yet promised not to and I know I am being punished now for it and I deserve it because I am fallen and depraved so I am not saying I don't. I am not saying Malone isn't fallen and depraved too even more depraved than me since I am being totally honest I am just saying well I am confused I don't know what I am saying. I will say what we said but I will leave out the cuss words because of clean heart clean body clean mouth.

91

When he opened the door which was much later and which waiting made my hands cold I even thought about leaving but I just couldn't I don't know why something was just keeping me there but when he did they were not there. They were not even in the bedroom or the bathroom because both doors were open so they must have jumped out of the bedroom window it is only a few feet but the way you fall if you do that you might scrape your knee which I hope they did or either it was a miracle come to think of it like God had made them never there in the first place which is possible because I believe in miracles and he and I never mentioned that they had been there so maybe he didn't know because God had already wiped that from his mind as a sign to me because with God all things are possible. No forget it.

And he said *what the H are you doing here*. And I said I heard you got back. And he said *who told you*. And I said well it's a long story but I ended up calling the dental school secretary and. *Did you tell her your name*. No I just asked when classes started. *Well you sure as H better not have told her your name and said you were checking up on your husband*. I didn't I sure as H didn't because now I was getting mad okay I was furious I thought I might have a heart attack it was going so fast. *Because I have a reputation.* I know all about your reputation. *Well what the F do you want.* Um well. *Are you going to stand there all F-ing night.* And I was going to say Malone I love you and I missed you and I just wanted to see you and I'm sorry for everything and if you'll just give me one more chance I promise you won't regret it and I'll get that money somehow and I promise I'll make you happy please don't hate me I know you're mad and you have every right to be and I'm so sorry but just please forgive me and let me try again I mean I thought through that whole speech I had memorized it but I just said this was a mistake you are a hateful person Malone I don't know how I ever thought I loved you by which time I was shaking from the cold but then I fell down and he was yelling things I can't remember like *you slut you whore you F-ing slut you M F* and I said shut the F up don't talk to me that way I don't want to hear it leave me alone and I just kept screaming whatever I could think of to say so I wouldn't have to hear him.

And then some more but that is all for now.

I am tired.

Now he will live with them.

I am worse than I thought.

Why did I do that what could have gotten into me what is wrong with me. How did I ever get involved with him I have ruined my life I am twenty years old and I have ruined my life I will either stay and serve out this life sentence or I will be a divorcée and nobody will want me and it will be a sin if someone does.

Malone I hate you. I hate you with all my heart. I hate what you have made of me. I have never hated anybody before in my whole life and now you make me hate you.

I am worthless I deserve worse than this but you are more worthless and you deserve even worse than me. Don't you see Malone that we were both going through the same thing we were both trying to figure out what our roles should be what kind of people we wanted to be I mean we were both trying to make a place for ourselves as Christians in a non-Christian world I can't say it right but what I'm trying to say is that we could have helped each other we should have helped each other because that's what marriage is for and you blew it. Malone you you-know-what you did this to me it's all your fault you will burn in Hell for this you will be weeping and gnashing your teeth and I will look down from Heaven and I won't even laugh I will say who cares.

I feel like throwing up.

*

How could this have happened to me I am a good person I live a good life I am kind I am all the things you are supposed to be. Okay I wasn't the perfect wife but I was just learning and I never meant to do anything wrong. Who am I kidding I knew exactly what I was doing take responsibility for your actions I knew when I drank I knew when I didn't clean the bathroom I knew when I left his socks under the bed. Why did I do that I said either put your stuff in the laundry basket or hang it up or put it in the drawer but I'm not going to pick up your dirty clothes off the floor what a stupid thing to do didn't he have enough pressure on him would it have killed me to make things a little easier on him but no I just left them there until finally he either did it my way or wore dirty socks how could I have been so thoughtless and selfish and cruel what got into me.

So what am I going to do where do I live why did I let this happen I feel trapped there is no way out because I hate him more than ever I can never live with him again but he needs me more than ever actually I am going through a hard time right now I sort of need him too. This doesn't make sense.

All I am saying is what if I just want to talk to him because I can't pretend that I never cared about him and sometimes I forget and I think oh I'll have to tell Malone about that. I mean I hate him part of me can't stand him I will never forgive him but I don't want to end up alone an old maid we didn't even have a chance to end it we didn't even say goodbye I just left.

I don't really hate him I would never hate anybody we are going to have go for counseling they can really help you and maybe it's good this happened because now we have to face all the problems we've been trying to avoid and we will deal with them. It's never too late. The fat lady never sings. We will just find a good counselor maybe Daddy's preacher since he's free and he would probably take my side and we will work this out and things will be better than ever like a broken arm that's stronger where the break was. With God all things are possible. I will just call him up over there and say Malone it's obvious that we need some help no Malone I want you to know that I love you and that it's going to be work but I know we can work this out I still need you and I think you still need me no Malone we need to talk can you come over. Maybe I'll write him a letter.
Dear Malone,

I know this seems strange, me writing a letter to my own husband, but I have so much to say that I want you to be able to listen to when you are ready. I don't know where to begin.

First, I want you to know that I am sorry and I hope you'll forgive me. I really don't understand exactly what I

95

did wrong, but I know that I contributed to what happened. Maybe it's just all the little things. Sometimes when I'm trying to go to sleep at night all the little things that I could and should have done come crowding in my brain and I can't get them out. It's like a cartoon and all the Jiminy Crickets are coming out from everywhere and multiplying saying, "You should have been more understanding, you should have helped him study for that test, you should have been more patient, you should have made more of an effort to like his friends and understand his world, you should have cooked better, you should have been nicer to his mother, you should have gotten the money, etc." But I want you to know that I really want to make all this up to you and I know we can get the money somehow. I am not holding back anything from you. I am writing an autobiography that I think I can sell for at least $150,000. I've read where people can make millions off of them and if they make a movie you can retire. You can have all of it. Just please come back and let us start over. I need you. I can't live without you. I will do whatever you want if you'll just please give me one more chance.

Where is my daddy when I need him this is never going to work I can see him reading this and laughing at me for being such a groveler and reading it to them and they all get a big kick out of it. I'm not going to beg you didn't see him that night I did it wouldn't work. So I have my pride. One of the seven deadly sins.

I am going to have to take control of my life if he wants to live with them fine we still have to pay rent on the apartment until our lease runs out so I'll live there. My mother is driving me crazy she is too oppressed repressed suppressed whatever I can't stand living with her I have no privacy if I need to throw up I don't want to have to report why and how I'm feeling now to her it's none of her business. Plus she hates Malone she's trying to push me into a divorce which I refuse I have my principles he may divorce me I realize that's a possibility I am a realist but I for one am not going to be the one to do it and then someday if he wants to remarry he will be committing adultery against me and against God and that will be his problem but I will be free to remarry any time I like and I will.

She hates Malone some things had happened like her yard got rolled someone threw a rock in the living-room window and prank phone calls these are teenager things Malone would never do such things it is utterly ridiculous but she was bound and determined to catch him she was upset about it all the time driving me crazy making all kinds of accusations worse than I have written so anyway I will just get all my clothes and some of hers and move out because I can't take it anymore.

It is better this way because I have my privacy and I have always valued my privacy.

Last night I dreamed that I was plotting to kill him and writing him a threatening note with a pen that turned into a knife and tore the paper into shreds and the shreds were his clothes. And then when I got to work today this actually happened I found this copy of *Mademoiselle* magazine in the kitchen and opened it and it had words and letters cut out of it like a mad killer would make a ransom note with on TV.

I'm not serious about killing him. I wouldn't do that.

I'm not just saying sour grapes either when I say I think he has a serious mental problem. That's the worst part about it. I mean I really think I could help him and he really needs it and when he needs me most is when he rejects it. In a sense his rejection of the person who is best for him shows how far gone he is. He is not his old self at all and I hate to say drugs when I don't know for a fact but that's what I think and I'm in a position to know. I think it's drugs and if he doesn't get some help soon he will flunk out of dental school or worse which is all their fault I should never have allowed them in my house I should have told him you can't be friends with them they are nothing but bad news and it would have been for his own good and he would be thanking me now. Now with my hindsight 20/20 vision I even know when it happened. It was practically right after school started he met them like the first day of school and they ganged up on him and he was too trusting and they gave him some and his personality started to change he turned mean and that's why he all the sudden wanted the money so badly they quit giving it to him. How could I have been so stupid I just kept saying that it was the pressure from dental school which indirectly it was because he never would have been vulnerable to them otherwise but I suspected even at the time that there was more to it than that but who would ever suspect a drug ring operating in their own house right under their nose so I said no it's just school and of course everybody says that things change in a relationship after you get married and I had no idea what that meant so I figured this is what it means he is feeling trapped so I'll just give him more freedom so he'll know that commitment doesn't equal trap and he'll come around. What an idiot what an absolute idiot how could I have been so blind. Now it's all perfectly clear but I swear no I don't but whatever I am innocent I promise I had no idea at the time.

chapter 21

Praise the Lord he has repented truly repented he is going to reform give up all his evil ways I'm serious these are almost direct quotes. Praise the Lord He has answered all my prayers He has given me the strength to forgive him He makes me stronger every day.

I have some chicken in the oven and he is coming home in half an hour and we are back together how could this be happening I don't know it is just a blessing and I know I can make it work this time because I am stronger than ever before. He called me at work and said *hi this is Malone would you like to go out to dinner after work*. And I said Malone I couldn't believe it. And he said *I guess you're kind of surprised to hear from me like this but I promise I won't hurt you I won't even touch you.* I know. *Well I've done a lot of awful things and I've put you through Hell I wouldn't blame you if you never spoke to me again but I just want to talk to you tonight I have a lot on my mind like I'm really sorry and I want to ask you to forgive me.* Okay sure I was practically speechless if I had been standing up I would have had to sit down. *I was going to tell you this tonight and I'll talk to you more about it then but I want you to know that I'm really sorry for everything and I've asked God to forgive me and I hope you'll find it in your heart to forgive me someday too.* Malone are you all right. *Yeah I'm just I can't explain it I'll talk to you about it tonight.* Okay and then he said he would pick me up at the office it would be like a date.

Then when he got there he was wearing a coat and tie he brought me flowers five yellow roses one for every month we've been married very romantic and I said come back and I'll show you my desk and I found a vase and put them there people will see them and know somebody loves me and I wanted to introduce him to Angie or Camille or practically anybody he looked so nice and he was acting so gentlemanly but nobody was around.

Then we went to this Chinese restaurant that is just wonderful I love it it is my favorite place it is called Mr. Lee's Chinese Cuisine and he opened the door for me and took off my coat and all that stuff I was amazed I almost felt like crying it was like déjà vu this is how he used to be before all this happened and all of this waiting and believing has finally paid off and I thought about saying it's so nice to have my old friend back but I decided not to allude to any of what has happened don't be a nag so I just said this was a good idea I've been thinking we needed some time together. And he said *I can't believe you are still speaking to me you are just incredible* and he looked at me like I hurt his feelings no like he was thankful I'm not sure anymore but very sincere. And I said what do you mean not accusatory just like please go on. *Well I guess I should explain where all this is coming from.* And then he took a deep breath and he was just about to say and the waiter came and Malone said *do you want sweet-and-sour chicken and an egg roll* that is what I always used to get he remembered and I said yes and he said *two sweet-and-sour chickens and two egg rolls. Anything to drink. No two iced teas. Now where was I.* Where all this is coming from. *Oh yeah okay well it all started when I got back from Florida that night no I mean the night before I left for Florida well I don't know when it started this is so hard for me to say* and he was sweating and his voice was cracking to show you how serious he was he was more serious than at our wedding where he was very serious. And I wanted to hear this and I could tell he was determined to tell me when he is determined he will accomplish whatever he sets out to do so I said Malone if this is too hard for you to talk about. And he said *no I'll just start at the end I went for counseling today because I thought I was going to commit suicide.* Malone how. *So I went to your mother's preacher.* Malone why did you go to him of all people and I'm thinking what in the world he will tell Mother everything what did you tell him. *I don't know why I went to him there was just something inside me saying go to him he will help you I think it was the Lord.* I'm so confused why would you think about suicide. *For one thing your mother was right I think one reason I hated her like I did was that she saw right through me.* No she didn't she was wrong about you and you didn't hate her why are you saying all this. *Well I went for counseling because somehow my life got off track and I was going full speed ahead in the wrong direction and I just went out of control and then today I got this letter from the dean of the dental school saying that I am now on academic probation and that I have to pull my grades up this semester or I'm out on my butt.* But you work so hard that's just not fair I can't believe all this is happening. *Don't get upset I mean I did too when I first found out I felt like a total failure as a husband as a student as a Christian everything but now I really think God is going to use this for good He's using it to bring me back to Him and to you and to almost literally scare the Hell out of me it's like the first shall be last and the last first I was last but God is going to use this to make me first.* I just can't believe what I'm hearing. *Believe it it's true but don't be upset that preacher is a really good guy and he really cares about you and he wants us to come in for marital counseling and I'm really excited because I think no I know we can make this work.* I just don't understand how could you think about committing suicide you have always been so strong such a rock Malone what is happening. *And the restaurant wasn't very crowded so it wasn't very loud and people started looking at me so I quit talking but then he didn't answer which made me mad upset so I said well.* So he said *I don't know why you think I'm so strong I think you sometimes just think I am what you want me to be.* No I don't. *Okay I didn't mean that to sound accusatory I'm through with all that I just well first I want to ask you to forgive me and to help me rebuild my life I don't even know how I became such a monster I mean just looking at you makes me feel guilty.* Malone stop. *I mean I guess the drugs.* Drugs Malone you really used drugs how could you do such a thing. *I can't explain it I don't know how I got started I just wanted to try it just once but then for some reason I wanted some more that's the thing you just go out of control so I guess the drugs had something to do with it not that I'm not facing my sin accepting responsibility for my actions and claiming the Lord's forgiveness.* He told you to do that accept responsibility for your actions didn't he. *Yes he's going to really help me us.* That's his favorite sermon. *Are you okay.* Yeah I'm okay I'm in shock that's all. *I mean well I guess I can't expect you to open up to me for a while but when you are ready to talk about it I want you to know that I will be here to listen.* Malone you're scaring me I'm so confused I don't know what you're talking about. *He said you would be feeling a lot of rage.* I don't feel rage. *Yes you do.* No I don't I'm fine you're the one feeling rage you're the one who wants to kill yourself I'm strong I'm in control of my life I'm just perfectly fine. *I want you to know that I'm never going to speak to them again I've told them I never want to see them again.* Okay whatever. *Please the whole time I was in Florida I just kept feeling worse and worse and so I'd just drink and get high and try to stay that way because I couldn't bear to be sober and think of that night and you and where you were and I got to where I was afraid you had been in an accident after you left or something and I was afraid to come back and find out how you were.* Malone just stop I don't want to talk about this. *But I have to I have to purge myself.* Well go purge yourself somewhere else I can't take this I don't want to hear about your drunken vacation. *I'm not telling you about a drunken vacation I'm telling you about a man racked with guilt who knows that he's ruined his life and his wife's life and who can hardly look at his face in the mirror without wanting to scratch his own eyes out.* And then our egg rolls came and neither of us said anything while the waiter put them on the table and he said *can I get you anything else* and we both shook our heads no and he left and I said can we drop this and eat in peace. And he said *okay* and then neither of us could think of anything to say I mean what do you say after that so I just thought about my egg roll. I put that reddish sauce on it and rubbed it in with the back of my fork and then I tried to cut a bite with the side of my fork which is almost impossible because so many stringy things so I used my knife and put the bite on my fork and tried to mop up a little more sauce off the plate with it and then put it in my mouth. And then right when I put it in my mouth my stomach turns into a rock and starts inching up my esophagus it's not going to let me swallow. So I chewed this one bite of egg roll maybe a hundred times more than I've ever chewed any bite before and then finally I made myself swallow it wasn't easy but it got easier. We didn't say one word through the whole egg rolls. Then our dinner came and after the waiter left Malone said *so how is work.* And I said fine. How is school. *Fine I mean I have a clean slate no more drugs no more alcohol and I'm really excited about starting over with your help and proving myself.* There's no such thing as a clean slate Malone. *What.* Forget it.

After dinner we came here and watched some old horror movie about these scientists who made up this formula that if you pour it on something dead it will come back to life even if it has started disintegrating so there were all these semi-decayed bodies running around and we forgot all that.

103

and here are the highlights

He stayed here last night no sex though thank goodness
he didn't even try he didn't even say anything when I went
to bed on the sofa but when I sat down to record this I felt
all happy and now I feel all sad. I have been doing that all
day back and forth back and forth.

chapter 1

Malone is right. We need some counseling. We need some order in our lives. We need something. I don't understand this but the sorrier he is and he is very sorry the less I want him. I mean when he was gone I wanted him back so badly it hurt to think about him I would have done anything to get him back but now he is Mr. Nice Mr. Thoughtful and I keep thinking yuck. I must be having a crisis of faith.

I know this is a sinful attitude but I can't help it and I don't care.

You would think I would be going panic what is happening to my marriage the most important thing in my life what is happening to my capacity to love and to respond to love but no I'm just going okay I'll go to counseling I don't care what have I got to lose. I don't think it will help I don't think it will hurt I don't have an opinion about it so I'll go. Why not.

It's really strange how Malone is all the sudden all gung ho make this marriage work be super-Christian super-husband etc. He is more different now from how he was before than most people are when they first become Christians. They get all goo-goo over the church and the person who led them to the Lord and they want to tell their testimony all the time and they take all these classes on evangelism and join a discipleship group and pretty soon they move up in the church and next thing you know they get on the decorating committee or the bazaar committee and all they care about is who can do the best needlework or the best flower arrangements.

We had dinner together last night and he said the blessing *thank you for the food and the loving hands that prepared it we ask thy blessing tonight and throughout our lives amen* and I didn't even close my eyes I just thought these aren't loving hands don't assume so much buddy. What in the hell is wrong with me I liked him better when he was a jerk. Then he told me how very delicious the spaghetti was and that he told some guy at school today that he was married to a terrific gal and a great cook and I just looked at him and I thought do you think he cares. And then he started in on the counseling again and I said Malone I said I'll go what else do you want.

Well we are going Saturday morning at 9:30 and then we are going out to lunch afterwards.

chapter 2
what I like
about malone

1. Cute.
2. Dentist.
3. Smart.
4. Funny.
5. Christian.
6. Ambitious.
7. Likes the same movies I do.
8. Good planner.
9. Good dancer.
10.

This is not much writing but I worked on it a long time. We went for our first session today and this is part of my homework. I have to make up a list of things I admire about Malone and then express all this to him during the week because a man's most basic need outside of sexual fulfillment is admiration. I also had to make up a list of things I don't like about him and then tear it up. That list was longer but I tore it up into teeny-weeny pieces and wadded each piece up into a teeny little ball and I'm not going to write any of that stuff again.

I also got a bunch of verses to read so that I can find out God's good plan for wives.

At first we talked to the preacher by ourselves and I thought that was all we were going to do but it turned out it was Living Loving Marriage Weekend: Turn Your Relationship From A Tragedy Into A Triumph at the church and Malone had signed us up for that without telling me. I couldn't believe. There were at least ten other couples in the Fellowship Hall when we got out and I said Malone I never agreed to go to group therapy what is this. And he said *didn't you learn anything in there you have to respect my ideas* and there wasn't time to say anything else. This lady named Carolyn comes up and introduces herself and tells us where to sit so we just followed her and sat. At first Carolyn and Kenny the leaders gave us construction paper and scissors and markers and said *make a nametag for your spouse that tells us something about them* which I thought is this camp. So I made this molar and wrote Malone on it and then we had to introduce each other to the rest of the people there and explain the nametag. One girl got a flower because she's so pretty my yellow roses are brown now. One got a heart because she's so loving. One got a lightbulb because she lights up her husband's life. One got a shoe I can't remember why. And I got a book because I read so much although I haven't opened one book since Virginia Woolf and not one before that since before we got married. Okay the one Angie loaned me but that doesn't count.

Then they told us the schedule for the day. We were

going out to lunch because that is on the schedule—a two-hour date and then report back to analyze how it went and then we divided up into boys and girls so we wouldn't hear what each other were doing wrong.

The Role of the Wife

Carolyn led the girls in a talk about submission all of which I have heard a thousand times before in LIFE group, Sunday school, wherever they get women alone they tell us this. Sorry bad attitude. It doesn't hurt to hear it again actually I even learned some things. Part of the problem is apparently I haven't been submitting enough to Malone. Look at any troubled marriage and you'll see a wife who is not submitting to her husband and a husband who is not **109** submitting to God. The whole Christian life is one of submission; being submissive to your husband doesn't make you less than him it just means you just have different functions. Carolyn says it's like a food processor and a microwave oven—Kenny is a food processor and she is a microwave oven (they are married); I hadn't heard this one before. Now I wouldn't give up either one for anything they are both extremely important but they serve different functions so when Kenny makes a decision and I think he's wrong I say what the food processor is doing wrong is between the food processor and the food processor's owner and girls the freeing part is that God holds him responsible. But what I want to know is how does a microwave submit to a food processor. You just keep your mouth shut and He will bless you for your obedience in spite of your husband's mistakes. When you're wrong admit it, when you're right shut up. Your role is like a support beam, make him look good and when he looks good you look good. At which point I started singing the Vidal Sassoon commercial in my head only the words didn't quite fit and I couldn't remember what the right words were. Watch out this can drive you crazy. If you adapt to him he will adapt to you. Mrs. Albert Einstein was once asked if she understood her husband's theory of relativity and she replied no but I know how he likes his tea.

The Problem: Why Roles Are Confused

1. Secular propaganda takes men doing women's work and they make it funny and imply there's nothing wrong with it so you have all kinds of TV shows and movies of the Mr. Mom variety.
2. Mom's income is needed or so we think so Dad feels compelled and again this is partly because of the influence of secular propaganda he feels compelled to help around the house and up to a certain point there is nothing wrong with this don't get me wrong I'm not saying that men should never help out by cleaning up the kitchen or what have you I'm just saying that when Mom works our God-given roles become confused.
3. Immaturity and bad role models like you might say my father was very domineering so I'm not going to let my husband do that and then you go too far and don't even let him be the head of the house.

The Solution: The Four A's

1. *Accept* him as he is. He needs your acceptance not your advice. You said I do, not redo.
2. *Admire* him. If you don't his secretary will.
3. *Adapt* to him. You didn't have to marry him you chose to and you knew what he was like when you made that choice. Love is a commitment.
4. *Appreciate* him. When he does something for you don't be suspicious be grateful. Don't hinge a price tag on your love.

Then we had to share one thing we felt really convicted about and I said I think I have been involved in a power struggle with Malone and I need to honor him as head of the house more. Carolyn said that was neat.

Then we went to lunch by ourselves. When we got in the car he said *well what do you think*. And I said I don't know I just wish you'd told me what this was going to be why couldn't you just be honest. *Sweetheart I didn't mean to be dishonest I'm just trying to be the spiritual leader now and make up for everything and I guess I'm doing a horrible job.* And I thought accept admire adapt appreciate and I said no you're not I just had to change gears I mean when you're expecting one thing and something else happens you have to readjust but that doesn't mean you hate the other thing but I really admire and appreciate you for thinking of this it was really thoughtful. *You do.* Yeah it means a lot to me. *Well that means a lot to me I'm really fired up we had a great session I'm going to be more sensitive to your needs now I'm going to protect you more I'm going to make up for what I've done* **III** *to you.* Don't say that Malone. *Okay subject closed now tell me where do you want to go to lunch.* What are you in the mood for. *I have a good creative idea it's a pretty warm day let's get some hamburgers and go to the zoo.* So we got McDonald's which was fine with me I never have put a price tag on my love and we went to the zoo. It was nice. We held hands and fed french fries to the ducks which is against the rules but we didn't get caught and watched the spider monkeys my favorite and rode the train and snuggled because it was actually sort of cold. It was fun.

I still have weird feelings about all of this but it was fun and he is trying.

After lunch we did some stupid activities like acting out a fight and a half hour of silent prayer. We should have stayed at the zoo.

So I just feel sort of strange. Like now for the first time he is doing all the right things and I have more reason to be optimistic than when I was optimistic but I have this knot in my stomach that feels like dread that feels like don't be such a sucker this won't last either. Which I think is wrong. I mean I keep telling him that I have forgiven him that I have been praying for this to happen but maybe I am lying maybe I still haven't really in my heart of hearts for-given him for something maybe I don't have any faith that God will answer all those prayers which if I don't He won't. I don't know.

But I am going to give it my best shot. If anybody leaves this marriage it's not going to be me.

One thing is still bothering me. How can I possibly submit any more to Malone and survive.

chapter 3

This just might work might. I mean things aren't too bad. One of the things he learned was Eat at least one meal a day with all family members present. Instill in your wife the real value of the work she does at home. I know because I read the handout he got. And he is doing it. He gets home in time for dinner every night and every single day he says something like thank you for cleaning the bathroom it looks really good or my lunch was really good. And I am doing what I learned and it's working. Like last night he brought me daisies and I thought Malone why did you do this they will just die anyway we can't afford these you can't just spend our money whenever the mood hits you while I'm sweating over the checkbook just so we won't overdraw but I said food processor and microwave shut up so I said oh thank you this was very thoughtful which was true and I put them in some water and set them on the table. This looks corny on paper but it's kind of nice in real life. So we haven't had a fight since all this started.

And I started sleeping in the bedroom again it took a sleeping pill and no sex just sleeping but still. And I might try to lose some weight. I am not fat I am still pretty I just have a little pooch. Maybe I would feel more like sex if my stomach wasn't poking out.

I don't know maybe things are great maybe I should be thrilled yes I definitely should. I probably am. I just don't feel things as strongly as I used to. I am getting old I already have some wrinkles. Not many but some. Maybe I am asking too much out of life. Angie was a psychology major and she says she turned down a scholarship to study psychology in Vienna Austria to get married what a liar and now she is divorced ha but she likes to make everybody think she is so smart and knows everything and she says Freud said he was trying to turn neurotic misery into ordinary unhappiness. Like that's all you get. Even the Bible says in the world you will have tribulation. Take up your cross. I have been crucified with Christ. To die is gain.

I think God is trying to speak to me in my dreams. I get this one dream over and over. I'm in the kitchen drinking a glass of water and Malone comes in and turns on the oven and opens it and I start saying no no you'll let all the heat out and then there are three Malones and they all have a casserole or something I can't really remember what it is but they want to stick them in the oven but there isn't room for all of them and I just keep saying no. And then I wake up. It doesn't sound that scary but in the dream I get really upset about the food and I wake up really upset.

I think maybe it has something to do with the Trinity. Malone being my husband, me being the bride of Christ, Christ being part of the Trinity (three Malones). Like maybe

I should open up my heart (oven) more and let him fill it more with good things (casseroles) like He promised and He wants to fill me with love for Malone but I am for some reason for no reason resisting.

Sometimes I dream about Daddy just that he is here.

chapter 4

Okay that didn't last long I didn't think it would I wasn't expecting it to.

So everything is back to normal. He came home for dinner and I had made it it was in the oven but then I had just lain down for five minutes because I had a long day Mr. Brooks is a butt I hate him at ten o'clock he stomps over to my desk and shows me the brief I had just put on his desk and says *did you type this* and I said the obvious yes and he said *do you know the difference between a comma and a coma you said the plaintiff lapsed into a comma* which I thought was hilarious but he has no sense of humor so I said you want a coma I'll give you a coma give me two seconds they don't realize I'm human so I took out the m and printed that page over big deal but he was in a bad mood the rest of the day because of one m and now I don't care because life is too short but next thing I know I hear the door shut and I've been asleep for a half hour and the dinner is burned as soon as I open the oven to check on it there is smoke everywhere it is a disaster. And he says *what in Hell have you been doing.* I'm sorry I just fell asleep. *Are you trying to burn the whole goddamn building down.* Malone relax it was an accident. *Yeah tell me to relax when I can hardly breathe god how could you do this* running around opening all the windows. Malone be quiet everybody in the complex can hear you. *Don't you tell me what to do who is the head of this house anyway* then he sits on the sofa and picks up a set of teeth off the coffee table and starts playing with them pouting grumbling loud enough for me to hear but not like he's talking to me *what do I have to do I'm busting my* **117** *brains out trying to become a dentist so we can live in Mountain Brook and provide a nice life for you I bring you flowers I take you out to lunch out to dinner to the zoo anywhere you say I pamper you I go without sex I do everything you tell me and what you burn my dinner you burn the food I have gone into debt mortgaged my inheritance to pay for.*

And then he picked up the daisies and said *why can't you ever throw these things out before they turn into mold and stink up the whole house god this is gross.*

And I didn't care. For some reason I feel like I care now just writing this makes me kind of upset but I didn't care then. I just watched I thought here we go again it was like that time he was sorry. Big deal. Big fucking deal.

And then he left his solution for everything and I thought good.

chapter 5

When I woke up this morning he hadn't come home. I turned off the alarm looked at his side of the bed and I didn't think anything I just looked at it like you look in the refrigerator when you're not really hungry just bored so you feel like eating but there's nothing in there you want to eat. Then I took a shower got dressed and went to work life goes on.

I used to like my law firm because you don't have to talk to anybody if you don't want to and you can have all the free Cokes you want. Sometimes people bring cakes or things and you can have those if you hear about it first and get in there and my desk is three doors from the kitchen so I always hear. But I can hardly stand it anymore too many

lost people it is really a bad situation Malone's mother says
I need to be a light shining in the dark but she has no idea
it's not that simple if you are light then you shine in the
dark automatically that is what you do by definition but if
you are a regular person what does it mean to shine in the
dark what do you do. I am not being blasphemous I would
just like an explanation of how exactly this is supposed to
be done.

When I got home which I half expected him to be here
but he wasn't the phone rang it was that preacher. He said
*I wonder if I might stop by sometime and catch up on how you are
doing.* And I knew it I just knew my mother had sicked him
on me I couldn't believe it but I can take it I was cool I just
said I don't think that's a very good idea. And he said *okay
I just wanted you to know that I'm concerned about you.* And I
thought objection noted and I said okay thanks bye. What 119
a leech. Some people never learn I'm probably just paranoid
but I'm serious he has been there wherever just there my
whole life. When I was little he used to do everything with
my grade Sunday school class and when I got in junior high
he got involved with the junior youth group and when I
got in high school he started doing stuff with the high school
youth group and then the college singles class and then I
started going to Malone's church half to get rid of him and
the thought even occurred to me now he'll start a takeover
move here which of course he didn't and I knew he wouldn't
the thought just occurred. And this might sound egotistical
but I don't mean it that way it's not if you saw him you
would believe me he is too short and dumpy but sometimes
the thought has occurred to me that he had a crush on me
not that I think he does but just that it's weird how sometimes
he seems to be worshipping me from afar. Forget it.

Then I ate dinner while I watched *Wheel of Fortune.* I
always win that game. If I ever go to California. Obviously
I feel kind of bored lonely tonight so I am just rambling I
don't have a lot to say.

I thought of something to put in my autobiography
today. The first time I saw *Gone with the Wind.* I must have

been four because I could read by the time I was five and when that first scroll comes on the screen that ends *A civilization gone . . . with the wind* I love that part my father read it to me out loud in the movie theater and he couldn't whisper his idea of whispering was to lower his jaw and talk softly with his teeth gritted and people were giving us dirty looks and I was starting to learn to read I knew what reading was and I knew you ought to be able to read and I thought if this whole movie is like this where you have to read it I will die of embarrassment but that is not the part for my autobiography that part is the burning of Atlanta. My father put his hand over my eyes and I watched the burning of Atlanta through the cracks between his fingers. In my autobiography I will make that very dramatic like showing the burning passions that I just barely perceived at such a young and tender age because that is what sells. And this is how literature is done. Authors find images like that to hide what they're trying to say in. I don't know why they don't just come right out and say it I do but that is how it's done that's how it's been done since time began and if you want to succeed at this game these are the rules you have to play by. Every summer in Atlanta they show *Gone with the Wind* on a humongous screen at the Fox Theater which is a real old-fashioned theater the ceiling looks like a sky outside it even has stars so during intermission you can pretend you're at a planetarium. One time this second or third cousin of mine who was adopted from Korea or the Philippines or somewhere like that and now they live in Atlanta her father is a Delta pilot and her mother is a Delta stewardess isn't that cute but she got to be one of the king's children in *The King and I* with Yul Brynner they do movies and plays. They would cast most of the children just for that city every time they went to the city and our cousins told us what it was like backstage the two little girls who did travel in the show were the real-life daughters of other people in the show who played wives and things and they were mean as snakes because show business will ruin you just like that. I thought about going into modeling I am pretty enough but I just didn't want to do that to myself. Plus I am not tall enough you have to be at least 5'6". So they gave me and Mama and Daddy tickets for a matinee performance and we drove all the way over from Birmingham just for the day it's not that far some people do it all the time and Atlanta is growing so fast pretty soon Birmingham will be like a suburb like Connecticut to New York only don't ever mention that if you are in Birmingham. Some people are very defensive about Atlanta they say we were the same size city we were even a little bigger depending on how you figure it up until about 1960 and then they got that airport which we should have got it was all politics and we didn't get it because our politicians didn't play dirty enough and theirs did and they got it even though Birmingham is more centrally located and now if you die and get sent to Hell you have to go through Atlanta. But I say hey this is the real world this is **121** how it's played. This sounds cynical but I'm not mad about it just realistic.

Someday maybe this summer I will drive over there just to see *Gone with the Wind* on the big screen at the Fox someday I will live in Atlanta and watch it there every summer if you watch it on video it ruins it Scarlett's horse cart or whatever it is is about one inch tall and the fire looks like any old house burning down but in a movie theater Scarlett is life-size or maybe even a little smaller when the whole time before she has been bigger than life and the whole room turns orange orange light shining in the dark.

chapter 6

Now I just feel empty and I hear every little noise even though I leave the TV on it doesn't help I wasn't made for this I feel like a reject I feel like a sucker but if he would come back I would take him. Some people wouldn't understand this Camille for instance who is a very angry person my mother for instance but I'm not going to be bitter all my life he made some mistakes so did I so we'll forgive each other it's better than this. I'm so lonely I don't have anybody to talk to cook for I come home from work and eat one box of frozen food and some cookies and sometimes I don't open my mouth until the next day my voice is going to stop working this is too much stress my body isn't working right it is not good for man to be alone.

There are so many angry people in the world. Camille is angry I don't know why. Mother is angry she feels God took Daddy away from her and left her a big mess and she doesn't deserve it so she takes it out on his preacher I have heard her yelling at him over the phone. Malone is angry because of money love of money is the root of all evil this is evil he loves money he is living in sin I wash my hands of him. I have been angry but I get rid of it because I am strong anger is a poison to the system it weakens you forgive others for your own good because if they want to destroy you the best way they can do it is let you do it yourself by hating them if you want to destroy somebody the best way you can do it is let them do it themselves by hating you.

How could a person be married almost six months and **123** already have made such a big mess of things how could anybody do themselves and the person they loved so much harm in less than half a year. How could you be such a failure without even trying.

I have got to come up with a plan. I will get him back. Please.

Or either I will get the locks changed.

No please I mean it please please God please.

chapter 7

This has got to stop and I am going to tell him I'm going to say Malone I can't take this anymore I'm not cut out for this I'm doing the best I can but I can't keep living on a roller coaster I'm serious I need some consistency. I'm mad as Hell and I'm not going to take this anymore. I mean I'm trying to do what's right I know I've made some mistakes and I've brought a lot of this on myself there's one thing about me I take responsibility for my actions and I'm not saying that I'm not at fault. Some. But God Damn It this is too damn much for anybody.

One day he is Mr. Christian Repentance I'm going to

Reform. So I believe him because everybody makes mistakes everybody deserves a second chance everybody goes through hard times I'm not perfect either. Plus deep down inside of me there's a part of me that still loves him that always will I don't know why you can't decide about that. Plus he means it when he isn't sorry he doesn't say so but when he says he's sorry he turns on his cow eyes and believe you me he means it. And then he proves I made the right decision he does really sweet things he brings flowers he rubs my back he talks to me he works hard and everything is very good. And then maybe I get antsy maybe I'm afraid of success that's what Angie says about her brother he is in this rock band and they have been singing for seven years and they finally got a chance to make an album they were going to do backup for somebody I've never heard of that Angie said was real famous and he lost his voice on the day they were **125** supposed to record. Maybe I do something like that subconsciously to make it not work or maybe he does but something happens and boom things fall apart. It's all fine for a while and then boom there's an argument about something really stupid and it seems like I'll never be able to forgive him for something like leaving his tennis shoes in the kitchen. And then it starts over he is super sorry he needs me he was just out of fellowship with the Lord please help him stop backsliding and I can't say no okay I'll admit it I like it when he is so sorry. I don't know what is wrong with me but I take him back he reminds me of a wet puppy and I say come in from the rain so I have taken him back.

But this is the last time. I took him back because I felt sorry for him but no more. And I will tell him that I will say look buster this time is the last time no more walking out that door unless it's for good. We are going to face our problems we are going to deal with them we are going to put this marriage back together and go on with our life. If something makes either one of us mad we are going to talk about it we can get through anything if we just communicate. I know you need me and I will be here for you I promise but you have to realize that I have needs too this is not a one-way street. And he will agree and we will be fine. We will start over at ground zero and build a Christian Marriage.

So I took him back I don't know why. Because he came back and he was sorry and he is having a hard time but he is really trying. Because I am a fool. Because I had to it was my obligation as a Christian and a wife. Because he needs me. I don't know. Because if it weren't for me he would have dropped out of dental school by now he would be a bum he would be working in the steel mills or something I sort of have an investment in him and I am going to make it pay.

The divorce rate in dental and medical schools across the country is something like three or four times higher than the national average which just goes to show that what we are going through is normal but we can beat those odds because we have the secret weapon of the power of God.

normal

Well I am pretty normal work is pretty normal Malone
is pretty normal hypersensitive about certain things but
that is normal for him his mother is pretty normal my
mother is fairly normal still paranoid about money but
basically things are normal. This is so weird. Normally I like
normal. Now even the word Normal seems strange. Normal
Normal Normal. It's not a normal word. Cat is normal. Dog
is normal. Plate is normal. Normal is abnormal. Abnormal
is abnormal. Abnormal Abnormal Abnormal.

When things are strange you don't have to keep them
that way you can count on one thing in life change. Nothing
costs exactly a dollar. Which is true but not the point I just

thought of it and said it. Everything changes. So if things are strange don't get upset just act normal don't worry they will change. A good motto. When life gets strange times will change. But when things are normal you know something's coming you don't know when you don't know what it will be you just know it's like walking down a hall in a movie not a big deal unless the organ plays and then walking down a hall being normal is the biggest mistake you can make because everybody knows but you that the organ is playing something is about to happen. And nobody knows what. I suspect one thing I'm sure I'm wrong it's just stress.

So you can try all you want to keep things normal but in the end you have to realize. You have to realize whatever it is you have to realize.

Cut this out you are driving yourself crazy.

We have teeth all over the place it is the teeth that are driving me crazy. Teeth and pictures of teeth and diagrams of teeth. You never thought teeth were so complicated. Everywhere I look teeth. But I'm asking how can medical school which covers the whole body except teeth be four years and dental school which is only teeth be four years and bodies and teeth have been exactly the same ever since the beginning of the world and even if they believe in evolution which I don't but even they believe the body has been the same a long long time so how much can there be to learn especially about teeth and law school the whole judicial system that changes every day faster than body or teeth be three. Teeth is another abnormal word. But I won't go into that.

Malone comes home for dinner every night. He studies hard he is doing better in school his mother comes over and makes dinner every Tuesday night I have started going to LIFE meetings again Malone is going to start going to church with us Mother got a job in a dress shop Malone doesn't mention the money anymore Mr. Brooks is on vacation for two weeks everything is fine. Normal.

＊

She made spaghetti tonight and we all ate it together spaghetti with her homemade sauce which there is enough left
for dinner tomorrow and garlic bread. She has her own garlic
press and she puts fresh garlic on the bread instead of garlic
salt like I do she says never take the easy way out the
Proverbs 31 woman wouldn't use garlic salt.

Malone ate so much spaghetti she said how do you do
it Malone do you have a hole in your foot. This is an example
of how original her wit is.

I'm sorry I wish I hadn't said that.

She uses canned tomatoes and I'm not complaining I
love her sauce it's just that if the Proverbs 31 woman wouldn't

use garlic salt why would she use canned tomatoes. I don't know why I'm in such a bad mood. She left her garlic press here. Do you think she was trying to give it to me so I would be more like the Proverbs 31 woman or she just forgot it.

chapter

I think Malone needs to go back for more counseling he is really hung up on something I don't know what and I just can't help him I mean I try I'll do anything I can but I don't understand what he is doing and he just drains too much out of me he is a parasite he wants me to solve all his problems I feel like saying Malone did you ever stop to think I have problems of my own. First of all he dreams he will sit up in bed at two o'clock in the morning or any time at all and say I'm sorry in that same tone of voice as that night he came over. Sometimes he just says it once sometimes a bunch and if he says it a bunch then he'll start saying I'm such a failure and I say it's okay Malone go back to sleep.

He never remembers the next day he acts like it never happened. Sometimes he says I should kill myself I'm totally worthless I'm going to kill myself which he won't he is just trying to get attention people who talk about it never do it. I never talk about it. But it just shows that he is depressed. And he isn't eating right he has lost so much weight his pants barely stay on and he gets indigestion so bad I think it might be an ulcer. Maybe it is drug withdrawal I know he isn't taking any now but he was.

He is also moody. Like tonight when he got home he slammed the door and maybe I should have just left him alone I probably should have but I said what's wrong. He said *nothing.* Did you have a bad day. *I said nothing is wrong just drop it.* I can tell something is wrong if you don't want to talk about it say I don't want to talk about it but you don't have to bite my head off. *Okay I don't want to talk about it.* Okay and then I started working on dinner we were having meatloaf I just hate it when all that grease is in the pan and you have to pour it out I can never think of where to pour it and it is disgusting yuck so I ended up pouring it into an empty can and the can is still on the counter I don't know what to do with it so I didn't talk to him all this time because I was trying to decide about the grease and then I said do you want milk or iced tea and he mumbled something I didn't know what so I said what. And he said *I said iced tea pick your ears.* Okay fine. Then in a few minutes I put everything on the table and I didn't even have to call him he just came and sat down and said *thank you for the food and the loving hands that prepared it we ask thy blessing tonight and throughout our lives amen* and I looked at him trying to figure him out and he just took a bite of meatloaf I can't explain how he did it but when he did it it seemed like a very mean thing to do. So it starts making me mad I mean I work longer hours than he does and then I get home and make his dinner and clean up the house meanwhile I've had a hard day too dental school isn't the only cruel world out there and it just bugs me that he doesn't think anything of making me tiptoe around him all night like he's the President of the United States of

America and one false move is going to make him blow up the world. So he's eating very angrily like he's taking all his frustrations out on the food stabbing it on the plate and finally I say Malone cut it out. And he puts on his innocent victim face and says *what I'm eating dinner.* I said you are eating dinner angrily. *Well I'm angry all right.* Not all right I'm sick of all this what is wrong. And he turned red I mean so red I thought he had burst a blood vessel or something and he picked up his iced-tea glass very calmly and I thought he was going to have a swallow before he told me and then he threw it at the duck at my father's duck at my entire inheritance and it fell off the wall bounced off the sofa and landed on the floor in a pile of broken glass and iced tea and I jumped up and he said well I'm just not going to repeat what he said it was the worst language I have ever heard in my whole life and it made me furious I was so mad I was **133** shaking I was about to cry and I said Malone that was my duck look you bent its wing why did you do that but I said it mad I screamed it. And he stood up and grabbed me and I dropped it and he said *that's right care more about your fucking bird than you do about me.* Don't you touch me let go of me bending down to pick it up again. *You listen to me.* No you listen to me this has got to stop Malone I can't take this anymore stay away from me I can't keep living like this I'm serious I'm mad as Hell and I'm not going to take this any-more I mean I'm trying to do what's right I know I've made some mistakes and I've brought a lot of this on myself there's one thing about me I take responsibility for my actions and I'm not saying that I'm not at fault. Some. But God Damn It this is too damn much for anybody shaking the duck at him the whole time.

And then the weirdest thing like I had hypnotic power over him while I was saying that he just went limp he turned into a wilted flower and he let go of me and sat back down in his chair and he put his elbows on the table and put his chin on his fingertips and then very slowly sort of dropped his face until he was crumpled up into a little ball and his forehead was on the table and his hands were sort of behind his neck and then he was perfectly still. I mean like he was dead. I could have said anything and he would have just sat there. Which is not like Malone. So I quit and I stood there without saying anything without moving for a long time just waiting.

And then it was the same old thing he pushed back his chair and dropped his elbows to his legs and started swaying back and forth going *I'm sorry I'm sorry I'm sorry* well I just couldn't take it. At first I was sort of frozen just watching him and then I had put down the duck and slapped his face and I was saying stop it stop it just shut up and I was so mad I was spitting every time I said anything. So he stopped and looked up at me with a totally blank face so blank it was scary and I said what has gotten into you. And he said *I don't know I just can't do it I just can't do it.* And I was so upset I didn't care and I said don't repeat everything you say now tell me what it is that you can't do. *Everything.* No tell me. *Everything everything I am trying to do I can't do.* Malone that's not true now stop this. *I'm a failure at school but I don't even care I'm not talking about school I'm a failure as a husband as a Christian as a human being I'm just no good what kind of monster would do to his wife what I did to you I just can't get over it.* Malone cut this out I can't keep going through this you are perfectly normal. And then he stands up mad again *Christ can't you have some compassion on me a person tells you he feels like an utter failure in life and you tell them to cut it out.* Well face it Malone you are wallowing in the mud. *Okay thank you for being here for me* and grabbed his keys and I said wait a minute you aren't leaving until we've talked this out. *I'll leave whenever I damn well please.* Wait Malone don't leave me. *Let go of me.*

He came back in an hour and went right to bed we didn't say anything we didn't even look at each other. And I'm asking you Carolyn what should I have done. You think if you just follow the rules you won't have any problems not any bad ones anyway because God will bless the marriage even when you make mistakes well I'm telling you it's not that simple. We have been following your directions for how to play Christian Marriage all this time but it is just a game we aren't really this way plus which we are losing. I know what you would say I can see you saying don't stand up to him keep your mouth shut you want God's blessing God's will more than your own His ways are not your ways His plans are not your plans why settle for your second-best when you can wait for God's best but Carolyn I'm asking you if God loves me why would He want me not to stand up for myself when Malone acts like this. I'm not being blasphemous I really want to know. I want to know what it means to be submissive if you say it doesn't mean you're less than him but it does mean keep your mouth shut then what. I mean I don't see keep your mouth shut in the Bible I don't see stay in the kitchen make him look good in the Bible I've heard it so much at church you would think it's 135 in the Bible and it may be but I can't find it. And think of Martha and Mary Jesus seemed like He liked the one who didn't stay in the kitchen who came out to listen to Him to talk with Him better. So realistically what could I have done sometimes your whole world starts falling apart and you want God's blessing ultimately you do but you just don't have time to sit around and pray for it you have to do something or it will be too late you cannot submit your life to someone like Malone is right now.

I am not making this up either I mean I think he is going through something like drug withdrawal I'll believe the best about somebody I love I'll stand by them until the end but face facts this might pretty much be the end. I've heard it can make you sweat and have chills and behave erratically and tonight he sat up all the sudden in bed woke me up it was so sudden then he ran and opened the window and I thought he's going to jump not to kill himself it is not high enough I don't know why but I went and grabbed him and I said stop it Malone and he was shaking like he had chills but he was sweating like crazy. Which I guess woke him up I mean I guess he was sleepwalking because when I said that he looked at me like he just realized I was there and then he put his arms around me and leaned on me I almost fell over he is so heavy and he started crying. I didn't know what to do I couldn't think of anything to say so I just rubbed him like a baby and said shh and maneuvered my way over to the bed and dumped him in it and he went right to sleep. And now I can't sleep.

I feel sorry for him I really do but good grief I shouldn't have to be the one he hurts and the one who comforts him because he feels bad about hurting me. He is a sensitive person that was one of the first things I liked about him but he has gone overboard.

I am not being blasphemous I just have some questions. Am I.

no more chapters
i have lost track

Camille had an abortion.

She will go to hell.

I can't stand where I work. Everybody is corrupt all they care about is money they could care less if somebody they know is suffering or needs help. I am sick of lying for Mr. Brooks. He likes to go to law schools all over the country to interview law students and stay in a nice hotel and have a fancy dinner and charge it to the firm and he does it all the time even though they know they're not going to hire anybody else for next year but I think he has prostitutes in each city he is no better than a traveling salesman. And after a couple of weeks some law students call him up and they want to know if they will get another interview or a job offer or what and I'm supposed to say oh Mr. Brooks is in court or he just stepped out of the office not he's sitting on his fat butt in his office smoking a cigar he just doesn't want to talk to you but I'm about to say that anyway because I hate this place and everybody who works here especially Mr. Jackson. You would think if you knew somebody was going through a hard time you would have some compassion and do something nice for them but no he doesn't want to dirty his hands with the scummy likes of me no he is too busy with get this Ann Barton which at least he could be grateful to me for. Everybody in this office cheats on their taxes and takes deductions for things like their phone at home or their underwear that they wear to work and that is horrible. They say things about their husbands like they cheat on them I can't believe they really do but they say they do which is just as bad in a way except you won't get a disease but if your motives are the same then it's the same in God's sight. I was never unfaithful to Malone even in my most secret thoughts. It's people like that who deserve this not me.

I hate it when people are typing on the computer and a lawyer walks by and they start typing faster and then when the lawyer is gone they have to go back and correct all their mistakes. I hope they miss some. Camille told everybody she was out with the flu but I know better I can tell how could she do it why would she do it does she know what they did they will cut it all up into little pieces and flush it out and then put it back together to make sure they got it all and it looks like a person it even has a sex what was hers. Or even they will take it out and it's still alive and they have to wait for it to stop squirming until they throw it away. It makes me want to scream at her. I would say go to Hell Camille but I don't cuss anymore.

I wonder if I will get cancer or AIDS or if I could die in childbirth. I hope I never have to have anything removed especially a breast. Angie went to the doctor for a regular exam and got a Pap smear and it turns out it was borderline

dangerous but they didn't tell her anything so she went back
in a year and had so much cancer she had to have a radical
hysterectomy the next day and she was only twenty-two
and had never had a baby and never will when they could
have caught it if they had just told her and she might have
a baby now but instead she is angry at God which is a sin
but she is so I am saying it even though I don't condone it
she is angry at God and so she sleeps with anybody because
she won't get pregnant anyway so why not I'll tell you why
not because she will get AIDS and die. First cancer and then
AIDS. And she did not deserve the cancer. Before it happened she was a nice girl.

Camille believes that she has a right to do with her
own life what she wants it's a free country but I'm not talking
about her life I'm talking about something else and sometimes you can't just live for yourself there have to be higher **139**
values. She thinks she would have killed herself if people
would have found out she was pregnant because she is Baptist
but I don't believe it. I would kill myself if I had an abortion.

I have thought about killing myself.

They have got to do something about AIDS. There is
too much out there that I can't control. If there is a nuclear
war they ought to at least make sure that everybody dies
instantly. I don't want to go bald and take twenty years to
die of cancer and first they remove my breasts then a lung
then some ribs then some intestines and bit by bit one of
everything I have two of until finally the other half of me
dies all at once. I can't do it.

They ought to quarantine everybody with AIDS. It's
the only way to keep moral people safe. And people will
have to stop going to restaurants which I have already done
not because I can't afford to but because somebody could
sneeze or spit on your food and they might like with Angie
if they're going down they're going to take everybody they
can with them.

I hate lawyers' wives. I hope they all go to some nice
fluffy restaurant that has gay waiters, get AIDS, and die.

I don't really want to die but if I am going to I just

may as well do it myself in a way that I choose on the day that I choose instead of being a victim. I will never be a victim again. You can't do that your whole life. At some point you have to say the past is past and the future is the future but the present is what I have to work with and I will not be victimized by the past or the future I will just go on today.

Which does not give you the right to kill someone else.

It is erasing but it is not deleting because you can't make what you have done and been not there anymore.

You will always wonder if I hadn't done it how old would it be what would it be like what if it would have become a lawyer or something or won a talent contest. And you will never know. What would it look like and you might and I mean might can have another one but it will not be that one because even if one is dumb and ugly the other might have been a beautiful genius but it is too late. Think of how different most brothers and sisters are from each other you just can't say how one would have been based on how the others are and if she has another one someday she will never be able to say you had a brother or sister one time but I had it cut up so she will live this lie with her living children what if somebody had done that to me would I have been born later or what if my mother had not married my father would I have been born to one of them or to someone else or never existed who would have gone in my place what if my grandparents had not had my parents like if the depression had come two years earlier before my father was born.

Where is he I was going to talk until he came home because time goes so much faster when I'm making notes but that is all I have to say and my voice is tired.

I'm not sorry I said it he ought to face facts.

chapter 34

Oh my God oh God oh god.
I can't say it.

I can't believe.

chapter 35

Oh God forgive me for I knew not what I did.

I really didn't I didn't know I had no idea how could I have known I had no way of knowing.

Everybody asked me questions all night the nurses the police his mother my mother the same questions over and over and over until I can't think straight. I don't know I don't know ask Rusty ask Claire ask his mother it's all their fault yes no yes no I think so I think they're drug dealers evil I don't know no I can't do this anymore.

I don't remember who called me somebody called me and told me who was that it's all fuzzy the first thing I really remember is I was just walking around the kitchen holding

my face and going oh no oh no oh no my hands felt cold
on my cheeks and then I started walking around the apartment looking for the keys holding my face going oh no oh
no oh no I couldn't find them anywhere and I emptied the
kitchen drawers the bedroom drawers bathroom drawers
took the sheets off the bed going oh no oh no just walking
around searching everywhere I couldn't find them anywhere
and finally I found them in my coat pocket even though I
had already looked there three times and I said oh no oh
no and I felt like I had taken five allergy pills like I was
about five inches higher than my body so it was harder to
make my body do things and my brain felt like it was outside
of my head and then I went down the hall and into the
parking lot and got in the car and I remember starting the
car and I thought about the fumes and took a deep breath
and I said oh God get me through this oh no.   **143**

    And then I was at the hospital and they couldn't find
him I said where's my husband and she said *I don't know* and
asked me all this stuff and I didn't know I couldn't answer
all those questions so I said somebody called me and said
my husband is here please just take me to him I can't handle
all this and nobody knew nobody helped me I thought they
would help me take me to him and I felt all confused things
stopped working and finally somebody gave me directions
to the emergency room *follow the red line to the end of the hall
then pick up the green line go up go down* I couldn't remember it
all and I started crying and I said I can't remember all this
why does it have to be so complicated so this girl said *I'll
take her why don't you come with me* and I said okay somehow
I had a kleenex and I followed her and blew my nose all
the way there and then we were in the emergency room oh
why does it have to be so horrible it was just horrible horrible
and I said wait I'm about to throw up and she waited but I
didn't so she went and talked to the people behind the desk
and then left and then this new girl came up and asked me
if I was Malone's wife and I said yes and she said *he's in here*
oh God Malone what have you done what have they done
to you why is this happening to me.

It was him. I can't believe.

God please let him be a Christian and if he isn't one please save him even right now you can save somebody who is in a coma a coma is a comma just a pause but he will wake up again he will either wake up here or somewhere else and if it is somewhere else please let it be with you I'm sorry I said I hated him I don't I don't want him to go to Hell he was a Christian and he fell away but please once a Christian always a Christian please be long-suffering and forgive him please don't divorce him because he was married to you and he left you for a while but he didn't divorce you and he wouldn't have he would have come back he was trying to come back he wanted to make a good marriage full of happiness faithfulness he just couldn't do everything please forgive him please have mercy on him please don't take him away from me don't leave me all alone.

chapter 36

How could I have done this I didn't mean to I am so confused I can't think straight I have to pull myself together concentrate what is wrong with me. I am all alone.

I gave him away.

They said *I'm sorry the third test came back negative.* I don't understand. *Well that means he is brain dead.* Dead. *Yes.* No wait he is still breathing. *He is still hooked up to the ventilator but his brain has stopped functioning.* Is he dead. *Yes.* He is dead and his heart is still beating and he would still bleed if you cut him is he still growing hair will he get thinner if they take out the IV feeding do his reflexes still work would he kick if you hit his knee this is too weird I've never heard of this

I've heard of life-in-death life-or-death life-after-death but not life during death.

I am not mad now I am ashamed I am horrible I am sad I don't know what I am I am a Widow. Oh help I just realized that.

I am not mad now I am a Widow but for some reason it made me mad then and somebody had mentioned earlier that I might want to think about donating his organs and I said don't be such a sicko but now I thought what a perfect thing to do I will just give him away I hate his guts I will give his guts away so I signed everything away.

I had his heart cut out I had his eyes poked out I said take everything you want as long as you take his heart and his eyes. And they said *you can help a lot of people this way you can help about fifty people.* I said just give me the forms and I'll sign. They said *okay first we have to ask do you know if he ever used IV drugs.* No not this again absolutely not he only smoked and he hardly ever did that and he hadn't even done that for a while he hardly used them at all it was Rusty and Claire they did everything this should have been them. *I'm sorry I hope it helps you to know how many lives you are saving.* Let's just get this over with. *Okay well let us explain so you'll know what's going on we're going to take the heart and the kidneys some bone marrow and skin tissue and the eyes.* You want his skin. *We won't actually take the skin we just take the top layer and we use it for burn victims usually children he won't look any different maybe just a little pink sunburned.* Just do it I don't want to hear any more about it. So I had him skinned.

I must be the worst human being alive. I am just thinking that thought I don't feel bad about it. What's the point.

How could I do such a hateful thing. Because I hate him. Because I am a hateful person. Because my life will never be the same. Because I will never be the same.

chapter 37

Mr. Jackson sent me flowers. Pink carnations.

The firm sent yellow roses. Angie and three other sec-
retaries not including Camille sent a mixed bouquet which
was probably Angie's idea cheap but thoughtful. Mr. Brooks
sent a potted azalea. And Mr. Ballard sent carnations.

I wonder how much they know.

The preacher is over here almost all the time. I don't
care he is just doing his job.

Our LIFE group and the people from Daddy's church
each have their own systems for handling this and they keep
overlapping so we have two huge plates of fried chicken
two platters of cold cuts four or five salads five or six cakes

and people here all the time. And everybody just asks how are you if there's anything I can do etc. and nobody not one single person has mentioned Malone. Like they just happened to be in the neighborhood with an extra jello salad in the car.

But his mother is about ready to have a nervous breakdown and everybody knows it but seriously I have enough problems of my own she has plenty of people to look after her. I am not being cold-blooded just practical. You have to survive and sometimes you just can't survive by wrapping yourself up in everybody else's problems.

And I'm also serious about this don't wear your grief on your sleeve. She is milking this for everything it's worth but good heavens when they leave here they say how strong I am it's amazing and they say she is falling apart what a pity. I haven't even cried I just think about other things I think about typing whatever anyone is saying where are the keys how are the words spelled and I think about reading a transcription of what they are saying. Have you ever noticed how little sense people make. Nobody talks in complete sentences people say he and I when they should say he and me and they do it because they are trying to sound like they know what they are talking about but they are grammatically incorrect that is what this world is coming to college-educated people don't know when to say he and I and when to say he and me him and me.

chapter 38

Well Malone what's it like.

Today is the first day I'll never see you again.

Today is the first day you'll never see anything again I took care of that. I'm sorry. I shouldn't have done it. But there are a lot of things right now that a lot of people have done that they shouldn't have done. Believe me it's dark where you are anyway it's not just you.

Yea though I walk through the valley of the shadow of death I will fear no evil thy rod and thy staff they comfort me what comes next surely goodness and mercy shall follow me all the days of my life and I shall dwell in the house of the lord forever.

Would you rather be in heaven with no eyes than in jail. I sent Rusty and Claire to jail I said everything I could think of to send them to jail because they left you. I found out what happened and I think you deserve everything you got I'm serious I don't feel sorry for you but they ought to be shot for leaving you while you're having a seizure what did they think anyway you don't call 911 and then leave. Oh well. Not my problem.

I just think it's ironic that's all. You're just like me Malone you never get away with anything. I asked the nurse why didn't they die too and she said it may have been an exceptionally pure shipment but if they do drugs more than he did they may have built up some tolerance Malone that's what you were always telling me I should do be more pure be more tolerant of them well that's what did you in it was too pure and you weren't tolerant enough isn't that great.

They brought me in to see you and I could barely see you you were surrounded by green you were sur-rounded by people wearing green hunched over you like predators predators working on you killing you working on killing you and you had on a black mask they made you wear a death mask to your own death and you fought and they fought and they won ten against one they put a straw in your foot and they sucked the life out of you your mother always said you must have a hole in your foot well you had a hole in your foot all right and your soul fell out.

Then they buried you Malone. They buried you next to your father and now that's where you are. That's where most of you is. Not your heart. Not your eyes. You are a fragment.

Malone how can this be happening how could you have died why in Hell did you die when we were just about to work things out why did you do it Malone why. I don't understand you bastard why you would leave me I told you not to leave me I was trying to help you. I was trying. I am. I was. You were. Am is are was were. You are not. You exist but you exist in the past and I am now. I feel you with me I can't escape you but I know you are only with me like the past is with me not really here because not somewhere else when not here.

Why did you do it Malone why did you do this to me.

*

God damn you Malone.

Not damn as in send to Hell fortunately for you that is not my decision to make I am just so mad at you I can't find words.

Why did you think I married you anyway. Did you have this private joke with yourself that I married you for your money and you had outsmarted me. Listen here if you had had to pay me to marry you $100,000 wouldn't have been near enough. Maybe a million maybe. I mean I don't get it some people would have married you for your money so if you wanted to find somebody to do this to why me I'm not such a prize. The thing is that believe it or not I married you for love I really did I married you because I loved you and you made a mockery out of it how could you do such a thing.

I am not a prostitute. When I married you the money was the farthest thing from my mind plus I knew you planned to use it to set up a practice I wasn't planning on spending it myself so why did you make it up. It's like our whole marriage was based on a lie not that it was based on the money but that you were lying to me at least about one thing and probably a lot more the whole time. What that's the thing I'll never know what. I just can't believe what an idiot what a fool I was to ever love you trust you give my whole life to you I would have done absolutely anything for you I would have robbed a bank and fried in Hell for it if you really needed me to. And what you are lying laughing in my face the whole time. I can't even say what you are. **153**

I am sorry about that first cussing. I am pulling myself together not cussing etc. But what you are starts with a B.

I was pulling my life together I was thinking okay what am I going to do now and I thought I know I'll take that $100,000 or part of it and invest it in myself. I'll get out of here and start a new life I'll go to Georgia and finish college I will be normal I will put a bulldog sticker on my car I will have a date to homecoming and wear a beautiful new dress because I will be able to afford it I will not live in a dorm I will have an apartment right next to campus and everybody will want to come to it for parties. Then I will graduate with honors and go to law school and make law review and put a sticker of scales that says University of Georgia Law Review on my car and I will get a job in Atlanta making twice as much money as Mr. Jackson and I will see him at conventions and I will tell him look me up whenever you're in Atlanta and we'll do lunch and I will give him my card.

And also you'll be glad to know I was going to use this money to pay for your funeral you had a very nice funeral if you'll remember nicer than you deserve if the truth be told so I asked your mother about getting the money because Mr. Jackson said since you didn't have a will everything went to me and I am so furious Malone she didn't know what I was talking about. She had never heard of it because there was no such thing.

I mean here we are again same song second verse having already spent part of an inheritance that you just made up out of thin air. Why do you do this Malone why do you do it what is wrong with you.

I wasn't thinking now that he's gone I can have the money to myself which by the way your mother thinks I was she now hates my guts and blames all this on my wanting the money I don't know what's gotten into her. And I don't know what got into me when I believed you that she was mad that they didn't get the money so don't mention it to her just be sensitive to her weak spot I should have asked her I should have hired a private detective but that is another story I was just thinking since I have blown every other area of my life at least I have the money at least there is a way to start over it was a comfort. And now I don't know how you could hurt me more if you had planned.

Does this mean I have to pay off your debt too. I haven't thought about that but I'm telling you Malone you can pat yourself on the head you really put it to me you can go to Hell.

Sorry not to Hell just get out of my mind.

What if Malone is in Hell weeping and gnashing his teeth. What if his arm or his hair has been on fire for the last two weeks and he can't put it out. How can he stand it.

chapter 39

I went to visit his grave yesterday. I drove down there and through that huge black wrought-iron gate black wrought-iron with spikes why do they have a black gate with spikes on top it reminds you of the gates of Hell you expect a sign that says abandon hope all ye who enter here and there is a sign which you can't read at first until you're right there you can only imagine what it says which you later find out is gates close at sundown why do they do that to people it gives you a knot in your stomach just to go through the gates. And then I turned left because I could remember looking toward the white cross as we drove up it is a combination empty cross symbol of life and grave marker symbol of death it says Christ is not here but somebody is. And without people there I couldn't tell where to go it seems like you would know but you don't so I parked on the side of the driveway about where I thought it was and I got out and started walking around reading all the grave markers I probably read a hundred and I figured out how old everybody was when they died but the only one I remember right now is

Lawrence Andrew Jackson III
December 14, 1987
December 15, 1987

One day. And I sat down on the ground and tried to read Lawrence Andrew Jackson III with my fingers like I was blind.

Then I started looking for new graves where the grass was still patchy and I found two but they weren't Malone where is he I never did find him one died the day after him fifty-six years old and one a week ago today age eighty-two people are dying all the time. So I kept walking around reading every grave marker until I got to a huge funeral five times as big as Malone's and I stood in the back so far back I couldn't hear the preacher I couldn't even see him just a hundred or two hundred people all dressed in black and I don't know why I cried I started crying trying not to shaking like I was freezing where the only way I could breathe was in little sniffs it was the sniffs that were making me shake every sniff would go all the way through me I thought I was going to explode and I couldn't stop sniffing even though I wasn't that sad I even felt good sort of because I thought everybody here knows what this feels like but I was crying anyway. And then some man about seventy years old came over and gave me his handkerchief and I took it I couldn't even say thank you I was sniffing too hard and he put his arm around me and I put my face in his chest and closed my eyes God please calm me down please make me relax give me strength please don't let me be crazy and I stayed there with my eyes closed spinning around with him patting my back until I was normal. Then the funeral was over and I said thank you and walked as fast as I could to my car over grave after grave like a mile of graves walking over a thousand dead bodies past a thousand people's grief feeling like he was following me watching me but I couldn't stop what would I have said. Then I got in my car turned around and got in a traffic jam trying to get out people were backed up bumper to bumper trying to get out of the cemetery and I checked to make sure all my windows were rolled up and I screamed as loud as I could louder than I ever screamed at Malone I have to get out of here God please get me out of here please I can't take this.

I didn't even cry at Malone's funeral. I don't know why all the sudden I decided to be so dramatic now I feel sort of embarrassed and I still have this guy's handkerchief. **157**

I don't know why it is the same graveyard where Daddy is buried but I didn't go see him I just didn't want to. I'm the type of person who does one thing at a time.

He died at 9:04 P.M. We were married 201 nights.

chapter?

[Damn. I accidentally erased this chapter while I was trying
to transcribe it and it was a good one.]

chapter 41

This is Chapter 41. The last one was 40. I wish I had said 40 instead of question mark but I didn't know I didn't know at the time and I had to talk right away not stop to figure out where I was and now I can't go back and redo it. You can't rewrite anything the past is unchanging unchangeable now I never rewrite anything what happens happens.

Well this is too much this is just too much if I were reading this instead of having to live it I would say this is too much. I would say how ironic. I would say this is very ironic don't you love the irony. But as it is I say this is too damn much.

I went back to the hospital today for life this time not death not exactly welcome life either I might add but there's just some more irony for you. I went back to the hospital today because there are certain biological facts that have to be faced and this is my new thing: face it. I don't know what on earth I will do about it but I'll face it first figure that out second.

I went there after work and I wore my wedding ring I still do that sometimes I don't know why just for fun mainly I guess. Plus it makes life easier. If you wear a wedding ring people will leave you alone if you don't they will flirt with you whether you want them to or not so I wear mine and nobody bothers me. I was thinking of not wearing it to work anymore but I will probably change my mind.

I paid thirteen dollars cash it really was thirteen dollars I didn't just make that up to show how unlucky it was and I told them a fake name I said my name is Camille Jones I don't know why I did that I just did. And then they said *wait out there* and I waited so long that I thought they knew and they had called the police for impersonating someone else and every time the elevator opened I thought it was them and I would say I'm not Camille Jones I've never heard of any Camille Jones I'm just going to visit a friend who is here sick who was in a car accident who goes to our church I'm on the Mercy Committee but I'm a little squeamish and I was just getting up my nerve excuse me and I would get on the elevator and disappear. But they never came so I just sat there waiting and I picked up a paper where somebody had filled in about half of the crossword which bugs me to no end I can't stand it so I tried to read I read an article about UAB trying to start or either they have started or something about a fertility clinic and I thought give me a break I know what goes on in those things. Masturbation. People taking God's work into their own hands.

And then this woman came out and I mean if anybody is a lesbian she was she was seriously six feet tall weighed about 200 pounds it makes you wonder if her mother took hormones or something she had a very deep voice but she was definitely a woman very big chest but there was something about her I don't mean to sound horrible but she was scary. And she said *Ms. Jones* meaning me and the way she said it my armpits started itching gross but true and I put down the paper and picked up my purse and followed her and she said *have a seat Ms. Jones* and I sat down I didn't say anything I just sat down and I had thought they were going to prick my finger how much could they need but then I saw these bottles and she tied a rubber string around my arm this gives me a stomachache just saying it and I thought why did I come here this was a mistake I have to get out of here I think they take more than they need and give it to patients but I don't want other people total strangers walking around with my blood in them but it doesn't matter what I want they will do whatever they want I may as well **161** be dead so I looked at the pattern in the wall concrete block that didn't last long so I started quoting James 1 to myself I used to know the whole thing and now I'm rusty on it James a bondservant of God and of the Lord Jesus Christ to the twelve tribes which are dispersed abroad greetings. Consider it all joy my brethren when you encounter various trials, knowing that the testing of your faith produces endurance and let endurance have its perfect result that you may be perfect and complete lacking in nothing but if any of you lacks faith let him ask of God who gives to all men generously and without reproach for the man who doubts is like the surf of the sea driven and tossed by the wind. Let not that man expect that he will receive anything from the Lord. I forgot some. Do not say when you experience temptation I am being tempted by God for God himself cannot be tempted and he does not tempt anyone. But every man is tempted when he is enticed by his own lust and when lust has conceived it brings forth sin and when sin is accomplished it brings forth death.

Only not this time.

I will find out between three and four tomorrow.

. . .

Malone you want to take responsibility for your actions well try this on for size. What would Carolyn say if she knew she would say praise the Lord children are a heritage of the Lord and the fruit of the womb is his reward bless the Lord oh my soul and all that is within me bless his holy name.

I sprayed for roaches last night before I went to bed and woke up in the middle of the night with a stomachache. But nothing came of it. Not that I wanted it to. I could never do that. My mother wanted to but either Daddy saved me and wouldn't let her or she just couldn't find anyone to do it. It was against the law at one point. Not anymore but it should be because what if life begins at conception and who's to say it doesn't. You can't delete that it will always have been.

I hate to think about roaches dying inside my walls squirming around first running away then walking then sort of stumbling not in a straight line then on their backs shaking with convulsions and their legs still fighting. Last night I sprayed one on the kitchen floor and he ran and I sprayed him all the way into the bedroom and when he turned over squirming I just kept spraying except when I stopped to watch him struggle. And when I knew he would die I just kept spraying and he was sopping wet and the spray was dripping off and I couldn't stop spraying and poison got all over my hands and my underwear that were on the floor near him and I didn't care I just had to keep spraying and then he died and I sprayed until I ran out of spray and went to bed.

When I woke up this morning my hands still smelled like bug spray. Even after I washed them.

It is probably about the size of a large roach.

I am hungry all the time.

Sometimes I am lonely too.

I think I wish I had not killed all those roaches. I had to sweep up three off the kitchen floor this morning and I threw them outside because it didn't seem right not to. There is something about something that is dead that is disgusting. And something about something so small. Like it has life but so what and if it is dead so what.

＊

Mother called tonight and said *how are you* which she is very nosy these days trying to find out everything there is to know she has changed ever since she started working at that dress shop and I told her so I said Mother you've changed why can't you respect my privacy anymore. And she said *sweetheart* because she still calls me that because she can't see that I'm not the same person anymore *sweetheart I'm just concerned because you said the other day that you thought you might be coming down with something.* And I said oh well a lot has happened since last week like I am feeling better I am taking vitamins I got a raise and a promotion and things couldn't be better I am taking charge of my own life I am a modern woman. And she said *oh how exciting tell me all about your new position* she is so conniving. So I said well I'm pretty exhausted right now but we'll talk soon okay. I do not need men. Or anybody. I am independent and happy and this is why I hardly write anymore I don't need to. I don't sit around feeling sorry for myself anymore I am a woman of action. I get a plan and I go with it.

As long as no one guesses which they shouldn't because it is none of their business but they will try to but I will outsmart them when the time comes. I can take care of myself.

I have done many things to take care of myself. Look out for number one. When I think about my childhood for my autobiography I think about my father trying to teach me to share you shouldn't do that to a child because that's not how to make it in the real world you don't go through life sharing or you spend it under a truck. That's what I did with Malone I let him take take take and from day one I should have said here's what I want give it to me or get out which of course he would have and I wouldn't be where I am today and it turns out I am having a few problems and I will have a few more but when it's all over here's a thought I could have had a free ride for nine months and be ten thousand dollars richer so I don't mind. Remember when I said I can put up with anything when I know it will pay off in the end this is an example.

I will buy some beautiful clothes really up-to-the-minute things maybe even a top with sequins on it and get my hair done like a permanent which I have never had one and maybe I will color it right now it is sort of light brown but it's basically a camouflage color I mean no one would ever notice it but what if it were a few shades lighter I would show up that's what maybe that's been my problem all along. I have never seen Ann Barton but I imagine she has dyed blond hair. I saw an actress I think it was Morgan Fairchild who I normally wouldn't take advice from because you can imagine but she or whoever it was said when she got to Hollywood she got a few jobs and then she started dyeing her hair and the blonder it got the more jobs she got which is certainly interesting but who would go on national television and say I dye my hair people have no sense of privacy anymore which is what's wrong with this world.

I could do this for a living if I could avoid seeing people the last three months every time. Maybe I could get them to write it into the contract next time that they have to send me to Florida the last three months I tell her it's business which it is and I'm home free.

I am thinking more clearly now than I ever have before.

I am finally in control of my destiny.

I am woman hear me roar.

*

Time is running out. I have until tomorrow to drink the milk
in my refrigerator before it goes bad the sour cream is already
over the edge although I could eat it now and not get sick
but I can't eat it because I don't have anything to eat it with
you can't just eat sour cream. My fruit does not have dates
on it which is trickier you have to guess there's no way to
tell with apples they look just the same on the outside but
you bite in and boom yuck except that sometimes they don't
even taste bad they're even sweeter so you don't know until
you look and then you see varicose veins. Bananas on the
other hand you can tell except they might go bad outside
and not inside or they might just have a teeny dot outside

and a bruise all the way through on the inside you just can't tell. I like them not to have any black dots on them only every time I look at my banana it has another black dot on it. It makes me want to scream. You just can't stop it. Dot after dot and the yellow that's not dotted is getting browner and browner dots and brown it makes you wonder exactly what does it mean to go bananas. I hate that banana I just can't eat it I just drank a whole glass of milk and ate a cheese sandwich. The cheese goes bad in three weeks and the bread in one. Why can't they make bread and cheese to come out even I can't eat a whole loaf of bread in a week what do they expect and yet they put these dates on them and say don't eat them after this date but they don't understand that some people live by themselves and can't eat as fast as they want us to. What if I don't want any cheese for the next three weeks. What do I do just let it go bad in my refrigerator **169** and then I have mold spores in the refrigerator and even if I throw away the cheese uneaten which is a sin because bad stewardship I still have mold spores flying around the refrigerator and landing on all the rest of my food so I have to throw it out too which makes as many more sins as there is food in my refrigerator. My crackers will last until the first of next year maybe longer than me and my canned food will last as long as I want it to. I am in total control of canned food. I will buy more of it next time I buy food. I have a can of pears that I bought the first time I went to the grocery store after I got married and I could open it now and it would be fine whereas if it were live pears you couldn't even stand to be in the same room with them. Canned is best because you don't have to worry about as much. I was married once but there was too much to worry about. Canned is best because no dots of decay no change no rot. You do not have to sin the sin of bad stewardship if your food is canned. You can always eat it later if you don't want it now. I love canned food. I love canned pears. I loved canned peas with a silver label even though they are more expensive than Del Monte. I love canned soup especially Campbell's Chunky all kinds except the ones that have ham. You shouldn't eat ham because God gave it to the Jews as a rule not to eat for a reason and that is that pork is filthy and you can get many diseases from it probably cancer. You should eat beef and chicken and fish and not drink alcohol because your body is a temple and you wouldn't pour wine all over the pews in a temple would you. No but then again you wouldn't pour milk all over them either. Which is not the point the point is that if the Holy Spirit dwells in you then you should not drink alcohol or He will have to drink it too and the surgeon general has declared that it might cause birth defects you would be born again but without an ear or something. The point is that if the Holy Spirit dwells in you then you should not drink alcohol or He will have to drink it too and you do not want God drunk. You do not want to be drunk either. Alcohol is a drug and it will kill you and it will kill your brain it will kill almost everything inside you. Alcohol is horrible. I hate it. Righteous hate. Alcohol has destroyed many lives. Possibly mine. He who has ears to hear let him hear. If your ear offends you cut it off and cast it into the ocean it is better to enter the kingdom of heaven without an ear than not to. Don't pierce your ears God did not make them that way. And God created ears. I have very large lobes and I have to wear big earrings to cover them up and I am not talking about long dangly ones that make you look like you are a prostitute just not teeny ones like fake pearls I mean button types that just cover up your lobes without hanging down. I have four pairs which doesn't sound like much but I am thankful for them because they are from the Lord. I have some that are 18-carat elec- troplated gold with blue swirls and they are round and flat and I have some square bumpy-flat ones that are plain gold electroplated gold and I have some gold ones shaped like shells not real gold although no one can tell and some black ones they are all very conservative you could wear them to the office if you were a lawyer or anything. Also an opal ring that my father gave me when I graduated from high school. They make me look very beautiful. I will have my picture made in them. One in each pair. And I will put my hair in barrettes or brush it back so they show. Two in barrettes two brushed back. You will not be able to see my lobes at all and you will think they are real gold and I will look perfectly normal. That is the miracle and the blessing of earrings.

*

I woke up in the middle of the night from this dream that somebody was trying to stab me and I was lying there thinking about murderers and I started thinking this baby murdered Malone which in a way it did since if it weren't for the baby Malone wouldn't be dead and I thought this is worse than Cain and Abel brother against brother this is son killing father and I thought of *Oedipus Rex* we read that in high school and I loved it at the time but I never realized how terrible terrifying it is. Being pregnant should connect you with all the life-giving forces of the universe I read that somewhere but it doesn't I feel tied to the violence. I still believe in creation I mean having a baby will prove that to you but I'm just saying the idea of a Big Bang is certainly interesting if nothing else it is an interesting metaphor of how everything springs from violence or at least that's how it feels right now.

And I reached down and touched my stomach and then I started to roll over and this sharp pain went through me and I thought what if the baby dies before it's born what if my own body kills my baby and then I'm a murderer with another murderer inside me.

Then I sat up and turned on the light just waiting for something to happen but nothing did no more pains or anything so I came in here to write I got out my pen and I could see myself tripping and the pen going inside me killing the baby I didn't even want to do it I didn't even consider it but the picture came into my mind I don't know why.

173

So I was going to tell the whole story what the baby had done what Malone did what everybody did but my pen wouldn't write I'm not saying writer's block I had plenty to say but no ink would come out so I started scribbling and scribbling scribbling so hard I tore the paper and right when I tore it ink started coming out in gobs the pen sort of quietly exploded and I couldn't help it it looked like blood black blood it looked like either the pen or the paper was bleeding and I'm not saying I thought it was just that it made me think of that which made me feel like throwing up. So I said forget it I'm not going to write and I washed my hands and watched *Love Connection*.

I decided to take today off. I called in sick which wasn't exactly a lie this is a medical condition and I am going to figure out what to do with his stuff. The teeth I will throw away I always hated the teeth I can't even stand to touch them I will tear a piece of paper out of my blue notebook as soon as I finish this and grab the teeth with it and throw them away. The duck I will put in a box maybe they could fix it maybe someday I will try to get it fixed maybe Mother will let me keep it in her basement. The books I will sell he probably has $500 worth of books. $500 worth of books about teeth. The clothes are a problem I can't figure out what to do with them I don't even want to look at them much less touch them. They feel haunted. Like his green wool sweater I grabbed it the other night like everything was normal for one second I had forgotten everything and I started to pull it on and it was over my face and then boom Malone at first I didn't even know what it was just a presence that was him not a memory not an incident it was Him. So I stood there with my eyes closed my hands over my head without pulling it down all the way thinking this is crazy don't do this and then I realized it still smells like him and took it off and threw it on the bed and I started shaking all over. Like I'd seen a ghost. And his underwear well it was his underwear. The worst for some reason are the tartan plaid boxers and the ones with surfers all over them I open that drawer and those are the only ones I see and they make me feel strange. I feel like used underwear. I was going to give him some with hearts on them for Valentine's Day. He would have liked that.

I don't know I feel like calling his mother and saying come get this but she couldn't handle it she would do like she did last week when I went over to give her back her garlic press a garlic press not underwear not an heirloom and she went to pieces. We hadn't spoken since I asked her about the money but I said forget this, life is too short this is a garlic press I'm not going to get all upset about a garlic press I'm just going to drop it off it's hers she can have it. She said *oh I forgot all about this* and she looked at it like it was a picture of a baby or an artifact from some ancient civilization and then she started caressing it yes I'm still talking about the garlic press and she started laughing and fondling it and I felt so strange I just didn't look at her I smiled and focused on the garlic press until she dropped it and I looked at her face and she was crying.

.   .   .

I don't know if I will ever have another man I don't know
I can't think about that. Probably not I don't know. I will
never go on *Love Connection*.

Stop. Now I am just trying to waste time so I don't
have to do the teeth.

*

This is all the baby's fault how could this be happening this is not the baby's fault what is wrong with me blaming this on a poor helpless baby. You were shaped in iniquity and in sin did your mother conceive you.

I just should have done it differently there is so much I did and could have done there is too much. I should have been more careful sensitive how could I have known he would take it like that. I could have built up to it I could have said sit down except that he was already sitting I should have prayed first. I should have said God is creating something good out of all this bad light shining in the darkness I could have presented it differently you can make a bad thing not nearly as bad if you present it right why did I do like that. Did I want to make him feel guilty of course I did I wanted to heap burning coals on his head what got into me that is God's job.

Maybe I just felt like I wanted him to suffer because I was suffering maybe I wanted him to suffer what I was suffering maybe I wanted him to feel sorry for me I don't know what I wanted. But he wasn't paying any attention to me he gets all wrapped up in his own problems when he reads he can shut out anybody or anything and I said I think Camille had an abortion last week and he said *hmm*. Did you hear what I said. *Sorry I was reading* still reading. I said Camille had an abortion last week. *That's too bad.* She did it because she's not married so the baby would be a bastard. He looked up. Do you think it's okay to abort in rape cases. He didn't say anything he dropped his book though. Do you. He didn't **177** say anything he just shook his head no and his forehead creased. Because if I were pregnant from a rape I might. He put his hands over his eyes and mouth so I could hardly understand him *what have I done.* Then I didn't say anything I just looked at him calmly except my heart was pounding so loud you could hear it I could anyway it was like the baby was beating on my heart it even hurt and he stood up and walked over to me and sat down on the floor beside me all this seems like it was slow motion and my heart was like a drumbeat or the *Jaws* music not like either of those I just mean making things worse and he picked up my hands and said *please please please don't do it please I wish God would take me before He would let you do that.* Why didn't I drop it why didn't I say forget it. The baby made me I mean I did it for the baby or my hormones made me why did I say it. I thought what if he tries to hurt me and he hurts the baby I was thinking things I've never thought before I was so messed up I couldn't think straight and now I can't remember straight. It was like he was grabbing me like I told him I might and he grabbed me and I said stop it Malone or like we wrestled and he threw me down on the sofa and I said stop it Malone are you trying to kill the baby and he said *oh God what have*

I done and he was looking at me like I was on fire horrified and what is wrong with me I didn't care I liked it power I thought he ought to feel this way plus I thought he would get over it. I thought he had more strength than that I would have been more compassionate I am a compassionate person. And then he walked over to the duck and he started petting the wing especially the bent part and he said *why do I ruin everything I touch* I hate it when he gets like this. And I said stop it Malone stop feeling sorry for yourself just cut it out. And he was mumbling I couldn't even make out the words just incoherent mumble mumble and he started trying to fix it to force it straight. Stop it Malone you're just going to break it stop fooling with it.

And then I grabbed his hair and I grabbed the end of the wing out of his hand and all at once pushed him back and threw it in his face what have you done you ruined it what have you done Malone and he just stood there like an idiot and I crawled over to the piece and picked it up and rubbed the feathers on my cheek by now I was crying and I was screaming louder than I've ever screamed why do you have to break everything you touch just get out of here get out of my life get out.

How could this be happening.

We could have worked things out. We were doing so much better. We were just about to work things out.

I don't know how I will handle all this in my autobiography but I am still going to write that thing. It's just going to be a little more difficult now. Although I think it has better sales potential. I may not have to kill myself now because we have the drama of Malone's death in there enough is enough.

I won't be as famous as George Wallace be realistic but I might be as famous as Truman Capote or Harper Lee they were both from Alabama.

One night before all this happened he came home from

school he had had a very long day I could tell the second he walked in the door just from the way he sluffed his book bag onto the floor I could read him like a book and I said poor Malone you look exhausted and he said *poor Malone is exhausted* and I said come over here I'll take care of you and he lay down on the sofa and I rubbed his back he liked me to scratch his back in a big heart outline start in the middle of the spine go up then out onto his shoulders down the sides and come together at his lower back then fill it in scratch everywhere.

I have to go eat a banana now.

I called the Life-Link center today and I said what do you use the skin for because I wanted to know that's all which I found out they use it mostly for burned children it keeps them from scarring as bad. What if they gave it to a black child would the child be white there or would Malone turn black. Same with eyes would his turn blue.

It makes me wonder all kinds of things like I think about Malone being one with fifty other people more than he ever was with me he is a part of them. Okay he is a part of me too only not permanently I will get rid of this I will forget at least he is not grafted onto my forehead so that every time I look in the mirror for the rest of my life I see him. What if I looked in his eyes today without even knowing it. Now I look at strangers differently I want to know have you ever had an organ transplant or a skin graft and if they had I would want to touch them because we were old friends and spit in their face because they were cannibals drawing life from the dead body of another human being and scream at them do you appreciate what he did for you he laid down his life for you.

I thought if I gave away enough to help fifty people it would probably be on the news. A few months ago there was a story about a heart-lung transplant and they made a big deal out of it but when all this happened I thought well this is more than that but it didn't even make the *Post-Herald* much less the *Birmingham News* or TV. Nobody knows.

I got five thank-you notes in one envelope today but they don't tell them who I am they just say *Dear Donor, Thank you for the very special gift you have given our family. We will always be grateful to God for the gift of life you have given us. We imagine that you are experiencing a great personal loss at this time, and we hope that knowing how much joy your tragedy has brought to others will be some sort of consolation to you. Please know that you are in our prayers blah blah blah.*

That is just one but they are all like that read between the lines. They feel very guilty they just want to pretend you never existed so they won't have to feel that way so they don't tell you anything about themselves they don't want you to be able to find them and they would have to come face to face with the person they owe their lives to. They don't tell you how they look or feel. They just want to forget about you and go on with their lives.

How long do you think they keep all that stuff before they give it away I mean do you think it's all gone now or do they still have for example some skin and if they do how are they keeping it. You have to keep the heart alive or practically I've seen them on TV running down the hall with a Play-Mate full of ice and a heart but like with blood you can keep it a long time I don't know how long that's a good question but if you are going to have optional surgery you can go in every so often for months before and donate your own blood to yourself. I wonder if I could do that. I wonder if I will lose a lot of blood.

If they can keep the skin this long what do they keep it in where is it what does it look like. I keep thinking of wrapping paper ashes in the fireplace when they keep their paper shape. I keep thinking about Nazi lampshades made out of human skin I wish I could see one. The worst is I keep wondering how did they get it off him whenever I peel anything a banana a scab dried eggs in a silverstone pan I think Malone and I dream that he is a Hello My Name Is nametag from church and they peel off the back and stick him on my chest and I try to act normal and walk into church but he is too heavy and halfway down the aisle I fall.

183

*

This is not really any different than what I have already done. It is just another part of him it is a mass of his cells and since he is gone it is my job to decide what to do with them well waste not want not if you don't want something you don't have to waste it. I will give it away and forget about it.

Angie's grandmother had a cataract operation and she was sitting at her desk talking to her mother on the phone which we aren't supposed to do and she said *how does she feel well that's just amazing okay I'll talk to you tonight* and then she hung up and said *did you realize that they can do cataract surgery now where you don't even have to spend the night in the hospital.* And

I said no. And she said *it's just amazing what they can do these days they gave my grandmother a whole new lens and she was home watching* Cheers *that very night.* I just sat there and looked at her and I thought okay I am handling this very well and she said *are you all right your face is all white are you sick* and I said I think I have an ulcer and she said *you know what you should do is don't eat any more brown bread only white and don't drink so many Cokes.*

I have an ulcer. Next time Mother asks I will say it's an ulcer Mother don't get me upset you just make it worse.

*

I hate this baby. I hate its fathers I hate what it makes me look like I hate what it makes me feel like I hate everything about it.

I thought it was a lie about the ulcer but now I'm not that sure.

You're supposed to say life goes on and pick up the pieces and move on with your life but I'm asking you how can I go forward when I am pregnant with the past. I am not married to Malone anymore but I am still married to Malone's past I can't take a shower I can't look in the mirror I can't find something to wear I can't try to get out of bed in the morning without the past being here in the present.

It's like I'm alone Malone is dead only I'm not all alone and
he's not all dead. It's like I'm being haunted by this what
this vestige of the past this intrusion from the past from
Malone's past not even just my past so he is dead only not
quite buried. I don't know what it's like.

It's times like these when you need to make a fresh
start. I don't say chapters anymore because at first I think
I'll say Chapter One I feel this need to start over which in
a sense I start over every day even when I don't feel the
need and then I remember and it seems like nothing can
start over until this is over and I feel like a slave. I feel like
I think I will feel when I get cancer which I will like my
body is betraying me. If I have cancer in my arm I will look
at that arm and say why are you doing this to me you are
killing me it's like my body is committing suicide before I've
decided to do it or at least not in the way that I've decided **187**
to do it I don't know what way I will choose but I know I
can think of a better way than that. Murder even. Now I
look at my stomach and I say don't get any bigger don't do
it and I'm beginning to look like a freak I'm all out of
proportion I look like I'm in a mirror at the funhouse. The
baby is the same way they know what they look like right
now I guess they took pictures of aborted babies. Think of
taking a picture of an aborted baby. Anyway somehow they
know and it is awful I try not to think about it the head is
huge compared to the rest of it and it doesn't have any skin
in the book you can see its guts oh help it's like Malone
has started over inside me he doesn't have any skin either.

*

Mother said *if you think you have an ulcer then you ought to go to the doctor those things can be dangerous.* Mother don't do this I am a grown-up now. *I'm just saying you need to take better care of yourself.* Well I'm just saying you need to let me take care of myself I don't know why I do that to my mother she says one little thing that if Angie had said it I wouldn't think anything of it but if she says it I feel like strangling her. So I told her I learned this on *Donahue* sometimes if you lose someone you love your body will create something to replace it like a cyst I'm not explaining this right but it's something like that you might get a cyst or you might get cancer or you might plant a garden that will do it for some people but the point is if there is a void in your life you either fill it with something like a garden or your body will fill it with something like a cyst and I didn't fill it with a garden so I got a cyst. *I thought you said ulcer.* Same thing Mother ulcer cyst cyst ulcer it doesn't matter. *Okay.* The point is this is just a natural part of grief.

I wish it were a cyst. Then I would have laser surgery they would send lasers in and crush it up into tiny little pieces into little paper balls lint balls eggshell fragments so tiny you could never put it back together again and then flush it out and poof back to normal without even cutting me up no scars no bleeding no pain.

*

Well that was a mistake.

I called this place that had a half-page ad in the phone book I don't know why it just looked like a good place the ad had ivy trim around it and it was this letter saying I know what you're going through it's very hard but I can help we will provide free medical care clothes etc. and you can help choose the parents and it was signed Mary Ann in cute handwriting the kind that if she had had an i in her name it would have been dotted with a heart I don't know it just looked okay so I called. *Hello Alabama Agape.* Can I speak to Mary Ann. *She's out of the office can I help you.* I just wanted to know what would happen if somebody gave up an adoption. And she said *I'll connect you with a counselor.* And I've never felt like that before I felt like you feel when you're opening your grade report from school and you know you failed something only worse because it is worse and I couldn't believe I would have to ask it again but somehow when the counselor got on the phone and said *this is Wendy can I help you* I asked it again. And she said *what's your name.* And I said I don't want to say I just want to know a few things. And she said *are you pregnant* only she said are ya pregnant she has a south Alabama accent not a hick accent but a thick drawl like I'm sure instead of saying y'all she says yawl and she calls herself Windy only the Win is more like We-un. When she talked I was trying to figure out what to say but also how to spell her pronunciation. And I thought well what can I say I wasn't ready to commit **191** to this I just wanted to know I like to be informed I just want them to answer one simple question not to interrogate me maybe I'll just hang up if this is how they are going to be. And she said *ma'am.* And then I don't know I just felt like I had to tell her like she had some kind of power over me so I did. And she said *have you had that confirmed.* Yes. *How far along are you* which was about to get to me this is more than I bargained for but I thought okay one more and then you're answering me so I said almost five months. And she said *what racial or ethnic background are you from.* White. *Are you and the father both white.* Which I wanted to say does this matter will you just answer the question but I said yes. *I'm just asking because we don't have any prospective parents for black or Hispanic babies right now and we want to be assured that the baby will have a good home.* Which didn't quite sit right I don't know why I guess I was just nervous also frustrated because she wouldn't answer my question so I didn't say anything. And she said *I sure would like to be able to call you by your name can you just tell me your first name.* Waiting no thoughts even going through my head just feeling trapped so I said okay call me Jane. Which she didn't like I took too long to think of it she never did call me Jane she just said *okay where are you calling from* and that did it I said are you going to tell me what I called to find out or not. And she said *I was just trying to determine how we could help you I can't tell you what will happen until I know your situation because every case is individualized.* So I said all right I'm in the UAB area. *Are you a student there.* Yes I don't know why I said that it just came out. *Does the father know about the pregnancy.* Not exactly. *What do you mean.* So I hung up.

Then I turned on *The Andy Griffith Show* and ate half a bag of oreos and a glass of milk walking around the whole time I still have crushed crumbs all over the floor but I was so upset I thought what if they trace the call maybe that's why she was trying to keep me on the line for so long she wanted to trace the call. They will come out and get me and get the baby and take it away and put me in a home for unwed mothers oh God I can't handle this why did I do that what got into me she was a vulture I mean she wanted that baby she didn't want to let me off the line I was a prize fish don't let it off the line and now she's telling the other people at her office about the one that got away.

It was the episode where Opie gets a bunch of dogs I forgot how he gets them it's not important anyway but by the time I turned it on he had a bunch of stray dogs in the courthouse and Andy had told him he had to get rid of them so Opie and Barney set them free out in a field only there's a thunderstorm right after that and Opie's worried about them so Barney tells him Opie you don't have to worry about dogs dogs stick together they take care of their own if one of them gets in trouble the other dogs'll take care of it. Now if they was giraffes giraffes are another story if a giraffe gets in trouble the other giraffes don't care giraffes aren't like dogs they don't take care of their own. Giraffes sure are selfish.

Then they went and got the dogs back.

And I'm asking you what happened to those dogs you

can take care of your own if when that episode is over it's over I would get the dogs too in that case but it's not that simple as Andy knew maybe giraffes really aren't that selfish maybe they just have problems of their own and you've got to figure out where to put them for future episodes and they don't tell you that.

They never tell you what you really need to know.

*

Everybody complimented me at work today or thought about it Angie said I love your hair like that you should have done it ages ago she has dyed her hair since she was in tenth grade. Mr. Jackson smiled at me in the hall he couldn't figure out what was different he just knew I looked better. Mr. Ballard said that looks really nice but for him that is a lot you have to know him. Mr. Brooks is out of town he won't see it until Monday. Malone wouldn't have approved but he would have liked it.

Now when I look in the mirror I notice my hair first. This is healthy this is symbolic this is my way of saying I'm not like I used to be I'm better prettier. I'm Preference Light Ash Blonde.

I am also giving my apartment a face-lift I am going to cross-stitch some things for the walls. I like living by myself. I wanted to see how long it would take for a chicken not in the refrigerator to go bad so it would give me some indication so I did and nobody put it in the refrigerator without my permission and nobody threw it away and nobody told me I was out of my mind. Three days before it is pretty bad. Which is strange because sometimes people wait three or even four days and you can go in a funeral home and not smell do they put embalming fluid on them or freeze them at night is embalming fluid sort of formaldehyde is that why funeral homes smell like that. You can't freeze a chicken then unfreeze it then freeze it back so it seems like not a person either. I wonder if people who eat **195** more junk food and things with preservatives in them keep longer.

I am going to tell Mr. Brooks I have this tumor in my uterus and they are going to disintegrate it with lasers so I will be fine soon but meanwhile I'm pretty sick and I might have to take off every so often when it acts up. And he will say you take all the time you need you're a brave woman.

I am going to read a lot during the next few months and watch a lot of TV. I will not go out very much. I will only go to work enough to keep my job to keep my paycheck coming in I don't care if they fire me after this I might quit anyway. I might become a secretary for a big corporation that will pay your tuition if you go to night school I might publish my autobiography and live off the royalties.

I will watch *Oprah Winfrey* every day I am home. Someday I will go on *Oprah Winfrey*. I will write her a letter and say my father left me my husband left me everybody left me and I survived. I will tell Oprah Winfrey how to survive how to triumph.

I haven't had too much time lately for my autobiography but that will change. I think I will read some autobiographies like Marilyn Monroe or Judy Garland or somebody but not Virginia Woolf so I can get some ideas. One thing is I will not watch too many game shows except maybe *Wheel of Fortune* every so often. Never *Hollywood Squares*. I hate that one. And sleep a lot because it makes me tired. Four more months except that I will drink so much coffee and eat so little food that maybe it will be less.

*

Penelope Penn keeps going through my mind but that is a stupid name it sounds like somebody who writes Harlequin romances not a real person. I just want to have a name that sounds interesting it should be long so if I'm on a list of best-sellers or something my name sticks out the farthest and it should be near the beginning of the alphabet. Barbara Taylor Bradford is perfect it's long it's near the beginning of the alphabet and it has good rhythm and alliteration too bad it's already taken. This way it's not so much like being naked it's like exposing someone else but what about when I go on *Donahue* and *Oprah Winfrey* do I wear a disguise do I want to be famous or not of course I do but not because everybody knows about things like my itchy armpits I am going to have to rewrite more than I thought take out the sex leave out Uncle Dwight and my childhood too boring and start with being married and it will explain anybody who reads it will see I will be a symbol the heroine of the twenty-first century I am ahead of my time. And it will show vengeance is mine saith the Lord if you do to a Christian what they did to me look what God will do to you.

Sometimes I forget that he is gone I look at the clock and I think all at once he should be home soon no he won't or I am about to eat dinner and I almost get out two forks but I get out one and getting out one fork feels like the worst thing that could ever happen to anybody.

I was minding my own business I finished work I was walking
to my car and there was Mr. Jackson. He had on shorts and
a Princeton T-shirt and he was putting a cooler into a white
Ford truck a huge white truck so old the white was sort of
faded to yellow or maybe it was just dirty okay you want
to know yes he has muscular arms. I don't particularly go
for big muscles Malone looked more like a runner or a tennis
player I am just describing what he looked like without
comment. So I was minding my own business and Mr. Jackson said *are you going to the softball game today* and I had seen
a memo saying softball season was about to start but it had
sort of gone in one ear and out the other or rather in one

eye and out the other if you think about that it's actually kind of gross but I thought well maybe but I said I didn't bring any softball clothes. *Well just come and have a beer and be the cheerleader.* People come in their work clothes. *Sure Angie did sometimes last year.* Okay I might come. And he reached in the front part of the truck and got out a xeroxed map for me he has a gun rack in the cab with no guns just an umbrella and I wanted to say do you always drive this truck and do you always keep an umbrella in your gun rack but how can you say that without being rude. I don't know why I liked it that Mr. Jackson would think I would drink a beer not because I want people to think I drink because I don't care what they think but because I like people to think they know me better than they do I like knowing more about myself than they do and I like knowing they are wrong.

Same thing with the baby Mother believes about the ulcer she has little nagging doubts or maybe I'm just paranoid maybe she's just worried about me but sometimes she'll look at me funny like she's trying to figure out what in the Hell is going on. And you may not believe this I can hardly believe it but nobody else really suspects anything they all believe about the tumor and sometimes when people at lunch are talking about diets I'll say as soon as I have my operation I am going to have to go on a major diet and Camille has a great one she lost ten pounds in two weeks and she says I'll give you that one little does she know how much we have in common her diet might be the best one for me although I am being very careful I don't think I've gained any weight in my arms maybe a little in my legs I can't tell I can't remember what I used to look like.

But the point is I was minding my own business and I realized I don't know anything about Mr. Jackson that he doesn't want me to know I just make up the rest like before I would have said that he drove a BMW if it had come up And Mr. Jackson doesn't know anything about me that I haven't told him I choose what he perceives about me. I started thinking how I am the author of my own life stories and the life story of everyone I know and I tell a different one to every person I know although of course some overlap but the point is I was feeling in control of my own life. And then I started thinking about this book this journal whatever it is this is the place where I feel like I have to tell everything I can be sound asleep and it's like somebody pulls me out of bed and makes me come in here and write and sometimes I can say I don't even want to think about that I'm not going to write about it but I still have to write about it sooner or later. I never had insomnia before I started writing this book and now I don't know which came first insomnia or the book I know one brought about the other though. I don't know what is making me write this book but that's my point something is making me write this book. It's like Wendy from the adoption agency something makes me talk I don't always have to tell the truth and I can eventually hang up but first I have to record all this stuff sometimes more than **201** I really want to say. Like the part about Oney and Boney that was very personal nobody knows that not Angie not Camille certainly not my mother. I still feel embarrassed when I buy toilet paper and the cashier is a man so why do I say this stuff.

I realized talking to Mr. Jackson he doesn't know I am writing a book he doesn't realize he is a character in it but the Mr. Jackson in my book and the Mr. Jackson at work aren't exactly the same. I left out things like he grew up in Montgomery he has a twin brother he has a cocker spaniel that he sometimes brings to work he is secretly in love with me. None of that is true but if I put it in here it takes on a kind of truth. And the same thing is true of me I am a character in my own book I have great power over part of me and the other part of me is constantly being manipulated. I can say I am 5'8" 110 pounds I was second runner-up for Miss Alabama and it will be sort of true of one of me but it's also sort of violent to say that because it eliminates the 5'3" 135-pound me the one who just wants privacy not obliteration. I can't explain.

So I'm not as naïve as I used to be I know what I am doing. Which is good and bad. Sometimes it's easier to be naïve sometimes life is too short not to be. Now I'm not anymore and it takes much more work I am so tired of revising and the worst is knowing that Malone wasn't the only manipulator he wasn't even the worst. This is driving me crazy.

I haven't figured out all of this but I know that it's related to the baby because the baby makes me understand this better. Not the actual baby but carrying a baby inside me. For example that somebody much more powerful than Malone had a lot more to do with this than him. It's sort of predestination it's a lot like predestination this was bound to happen because it happened so in a sense I shouldn't blame them they are as much victims as me. I will not try to get them out of jail though because that was predestined too and even if you're predestined to do something and you do it and it's wrong you still have to pay the consequences. Think about Judas. This baby is forming inside of me and whether I like it or not I am participating in that creation and soon despite all my efforts and desires to the contrary I will have created a human being of course God will have more than me but I will have been in there too I forgot my point but this is all related I just can't explain how.

Maybe it's like the baby is already a person inside my mind maybe the baby is making me tell its story everybody needs a story to be legitimate your story is your whole parents your mother and father are only part of that whole. I know this is not making sense but I am not losing my mind I am just not very good at explaining partially because I don't understand.

Now the baby is kicking like crazy. Either that or I have gas.

Sometimes like right now it puts its head or its foot in my heart and I can't breathe I think it is ready to come I think it is too big it feels uncomfortable it needs more space sometimes it fidgets moving around and around trying to get comfortable but it can't. I think it will come early.

Or what if I've been pregnant longer than I thought.

*

I am almost finished I am closer to being finished than I
thought I have to start making some plans so I went to
the library and I checked out *The Writer's Market* because
I wanted to find an agent and that's where I read they
don't want autobiographies unless you are famous this is
catch-22 I would be famous if they would just publish
my autobiography. Well at first you can imagine I was
pretty upset I just sat there looking at the page that said
that wanting to tear it out except the librarian was staring
at me people stare at me all the time now plus it would
make too much noise and I'm sitting there and I think
it's all been a waste well at least I can stop now there's

no point in going on and then I thought what next maybe I'll kill myself I haven't thought that in a while but I thought it and it wasn't despair it was more like there's an option. And I decided to list all my options. Here is what I came up with:

1. Kill myself now.
2. Kill myself after the baby.
3. Finish it anyway then decide.
4. Publish it myself.
5. Revolutionize the writing market.
6. Become famous first.

All of which I eliminated as soon as I thought of them for different but obvious reasons. You can't kill yourself if you are pregnant because that would be murder too and I am a **205** lot of things but I am not a murderer murderess it's funny how murderess and mistress sound alike. You can't kill yourself after you've had a baby if your great-grandfather grandfather and father and the baby's father did or you will make it inevitable that the baby will too you have to break the chain. Even if you give a baby up for adoption which I may or may not you are not just yourself anymore part of you is somebody's mother and your life will never be the same. You can't finish it anyway and then decide that doesn't solve anything that is not facing your problems and I face mine. I can't afford to publish it myself and the other two are just not possible I can't become famous first I can't revolutionize the writing market but somebody ought to.

And then I thought of number 7 lucky number 7:

7. Publish it as a novel.

So I will call it a novel it practically is anyway. And now I will put a statement in the front saying all characters and events in this book are fictitious any resemblance to actual people or events is purely accidental. And I will have to go back and change everybody's names this way I won't get sued I will name somebody Camille I love that name it is the name of somebody with dark hair and dark eyes but not Oriental or Indian or anything just that maybe their family used to be Italian and now they are Southerners so they decided to name their baby like a Southern belle because camellias are the Alabama state flower and she has a veneer of Southern gentility but underneath she is a snake. I know who I will call Camille. Maybe I will call him Bartholomew. Bart. No probably not. I will have to come up with names for everybody I am not very good at that I can't even think of a name for myself or a name for the baby or a name for the book. Maybe I will pick a TV show and name everybody after people on the show. No.

*

This has solved a lot of problems I feel more in control of my life than I have felt in a lifetime. I called Wendy back only I disguised my voice and they said *hello Alabama Agape.* And I said in my business voice yes may I speak to Wendy please. *Hold please. This is We-undy.* Hello Wendy I'm writing a novel in which one of my characters is considering giving up a baby for adoption may I ask you a few questions about what she might experience. *Sure.* Well first of all she is six or seven months pregnant and she hasn't been to see a doctor except for the pregnancy test is that going to cause any problems. *Well it could I mean it's pretty important to have a doctor monitoring your progress making sure there aren't any problems.* Yes but I'm just asking if it would be realistic to expect that she *could* have a normal delivery and birth. *Okay I guess so people did it for centuries I mean if there are problems they're obviously not going to get solved but I guess not going to the doctor won't necessarily cause problems.* Uh-huh. *Actually pretty many of the girls do it that way I just don't want to sound like I'm recommending that.* Okay what would happen if at six or seven months she called you and said I'm pregnant and I think I want to give up my baby for adoption. *First we would try to get her to come in for counseling we would assign a social worker to her and the social worker would offer to come pick her up.* What if she didn't want to do that. *Well we couldn't make her obviously but we would try to encourage her at least and we would try to get her to go to the doctor for a checkup.* Okay but my character really can't afford doctor's visits. *Oh we would provide free medical care maternity clothes even housing if she needs it.* What if she just didn't want to do all that but when she had the baby then she gave it up for adoption. *Yes that happens too.* I mean would you still pay for it. *Yes.* Would you also pay her the money you would have spent on doctor's bills and clothes. *No it doesn't work that way.* She was thinking that sometimes it does she's heard of people making money off of adoptions. *Well sometimes that does happen but not with legitimate adoption agencies that would have to be done through a private adoption.* Okay that's where I guess I need to do this research for my book can you direct me to somebody who does private adoptions. *I don't know of any.*

*

I will write the baby a letter and put it in its file so if I am dead when it tries to find me it will know certain things.

How do you start a letter like that you can't say Dear Baby it sounds too much like Dear Abby plus it won't be a baby by then. You can't say Dear Son/Daughter too impersonal. To whom it may concern. Dear John. Because I will be giving up the right to name my own child.

I will tell it don't ever kill yourself if you can avoid that you should be all right. Your great-great-grandfather and your great-grandfather started it all they shot each other your grandfather drowned himself your father OD'd on cocaine I hope you are not a boy or you are doomed. Your great-great-grandmother moved in with her daughter farmed all through the depression I don't know how she died I don't know how your great-great-granddaddy lived I don't know how she died. Your great-grandmother worked as a secretary for the USO during World War II and raised my daddy. Then she went insane. Your grandmamas and me it's too early to say and I don't know about your daddy's family what people die of except him of course and your granddaddy they say it was a car accident but I bet he was drunk which makes it not quite so much an accident if you know what I mean. But you can see my point especially if you are a boy suicide is the thing to watch out for. Your Uncle Dwight great-uncle my mama's brother he is an alcoholic he will probably commit suicide that way but other people in our family second cousins and that type of thing they tend to get cancer. A. A. and Jackie your great-grandmother's little brother and sister they live in North Carolina now they both have cancer Mama says every time the phone rings something in the back of her head says A. A.'s dead his is worse. Uncle Dwight had a wife and a daughter one time but they moved up north New York I think so they don't count. And there are other people that I hear about but I don't know the exact relationship but it seems like it's always cancer A. A. and Jackie smoked in fact they still do. The bright side of this is that if you can avoid suicide and cancer you will probably live until you're a hundred nothing else kills people in this family.

I hope you have been brought up in a Christian home have you ever read Deuteronomy there are certain things that a person can do that will put a curse on the family for the next ten generations well you can bet that I expect that's what happened. I am going to ask God to break the curse in your case to count you in your other family if they are blessed or just to make an exception in your case if they are cursed too. Sometimes He will do that. He is very complex don't believe everything you are taught about Him get to know Him yourself. I can't tell you too much about Him I am just now starting to do that but I think it's good advice.

Also try to be tough I don't mean macho the men in your family commit suicide the women either develop a thick skin or go insane. I have tried both I don't know which one I will end up as.

This doesn't sound too motherly does it. That is one reason I put you up for adoption I wouldn't be a very good mother right now. There are other reasons too maybe we will meet someday maybe I will tell you then that is not a promise we'll see. That sounds pretty motherly.

As I write this I feel you moving inside me and I know that you are almost ready that our time is almost up and I am rubbing you through my skin which seems to calm you down. I didn't give you up without even knowing you at all. I hope if you are a girl someday you have a baby and a good husband and that you have compassion. You can be tough and compassionate try to be both. If you find some- **211** body that you can love and submit yourself to make sure that he does both of those for you. The Bible says husbands love your wives and wives submit yourselves to your hus- bands but I think it works both ways like wives also love your husbands and husbands also submit yourselves to your wives. I think it means love isn't stubborn not love is a fool. Maybe I don't have the right to tell you this kind of thing since I gave you up I don't even have the right to name you. I hope you have a nice name I hope you like your name. I never liked mine.

I wanted to tell you about myself in case when you try to find me I am dead. I was very smart the first girl in my family to go to college. I wanted to be a lawyer. I was also pretty. I imagine you are beautiful your father was very handsome. If you are tall that's from him. I was a pretty good cook my best thing was chocolate desserts if you ever come visit me I will make you my triple chocolate cake. You just kicked I guess you like that. I liked to read my favorite poet in college was Tennyson and my favorite novel- ist was Hardy I read *Tess of the D'Urbervilles* twice. My favorite Bible verse is Philippians 4:13 but there is another one that I will pray for you.

The Lord bless thee, and keep thee: The Lord make his face shine upon thee, and be gracious unto thee: The Lord lift up his countenance upon thee, and give thee peace. (Numbers 6:24–26.)

I will pray that for me too.

I hope you love your new mother. I will make sure that she loves you. I hope you go to college and become a doctor or a lawyer. Please don't become a dentist. I hope you are happy.

I have tried more than once to stop writing this book I have
said this is too painful don't make me go on but that doesn't
seem to work the book has gotten away from me it has its
own will its own life. Why do I keep doing this I say I have
had it I will not participate anymore I am not going to say
another word talking the whole time sometimes I talk faster
than I can think and I have to rewind and listen to my
thoughts before I even know what they are like going down-
hill on a bicycle I start and I can't stop. I am speaking against
my will I can disclaim it all later and I will this was done
under duress. I have tried to gain some editorial control I
have said start over rewrite leave certain things out let me

have my dignity but something makes me leave it in once it is written it cannot be erased. Those were abortive attempts they weren't well written they don't even have punctuation and they will come back to haunt it half the things I said weren't even true and from now on even less than that will be true. Because I've realized that you can make me write and you will keep whatever I write but I'm the only one who knows this story so if I'm at your mercy well from now on you're also at mine.

Malone is not really dead he didn't really rape me I just made all that up because I'm pregnant with Mr. Jackson's baby. Ha. Do you believe this you're not sure are you.

I refuse to participate this goes against everything I believe in truth honesty sincerity. This is not fair this is like what the Nazis did this is playing God you think you can give and take life as you please well you can't. Not for long. God is long-suffering and you could repent right now and I suggest you do because I would like to remind you He has His limits and you think about this you think about Virginia Woolf and Ernest Hemingway and you think about Hitler what do they have in common. I'll tell you what they all tried to play God they all thought they could make the kinds of decisions only God can make and they all got away with it for a while but in the end they all committed suicide.

There are specific laws in the Bible about how to treat widows there are specific things you have to do but what they all boil down to is be nice to them us don't take advantage help them when they need help not this. Look at what you have done to my self-image I was doing very well I was getting over this I have gone through many trials and tribulations but I was coming out of that into victory or so I thought and now what I cannot even explain my outrage. Okay for example when I thought about getting cancer in my arm I looked at my arm and I imagined how I would feel if it had cancer this is a very personal thing. Well this is what gets me I wasn't even looking at my own arm it was your arm you can take credit for all this I don't care about the credit you don't even have to reveal my name but I will beat on your heart you know the queasiness you feel in your stomach right now the confusion the unformed questions. That's me. And I won't leave you alone I won't shut up I won't give you any peace and I will call on God to protect me from you and He will not only protect me from you He will protect me through you you will take care of me in spite of yourself you only think you are my creator but I know the man who created us both and He is not going to like this one bit.

I thought circumstances were the enemy I thought Satan was the enemy but now I know. You are the enemy.

Who are you what do you look like.

That whole last section was a hormonal imbalance due to the pregnancy please ignore it. I am fine now.

I haven't had any cravings for strange food just strange emotions.

Why haven't I been to the doctor what is wrong with me this is not just my life I'm dealing with I don't think I have the right to deprive someone else of medical care just because I don't want to go. Why I don't go to the doctor:

1. I can't afford it I still have to pay some of Malone's bills.
2. They can't help you look how much good they did for Daddy and Malone.
3. I think if I have trouble I deserve it. This doesn't make sense but it came into my mind so I'm saying it. Eve's curse.
4. Predestination. It's all up to God anyway.

I think I will die in childbirth. I have dreamed about it the baby comes out and for a second it's normal and everybody is holding their breath waiting for it to take its first breath and then it does it takes a big huge breath it breathes me in and devours me. Or the baby comes out and then the afterbirth comes out and then they can't stop it my intestines come out my kidneys come out my heart comes out every- **217** thing comes out and then my soul falls out and my empty skin withers and flattens on the operating table.

I still dream about Malone all the doctors and nurses around him and then I scream let me see my husband and they all turn around and look at me and they are ants on a crumb.

There is only so much one person can handle and I am handling just about everything I can. So if I don't want to go to the doctor I don't have to I will go soon enough.

Meanwhile I keep the apartment clean in case I die when it comes and people come back here afterwards. Yesterday I decided to wash the sheets and I realized I haven't washed the mattress cover in a long time actually maybe never so I took it off and the mattress was filthy what did you spill Malone and I got a wet washcloth and started scrubbing the spots how do you wash a mattress thinking this is how it's going to be isn't it Malone for the rest of my life you'll be jumping out from behind doors at me I was furious scrubbing so hard I worked up a sweat. And part of me said don't get so upset this is just hormones relax. So part of me was furiously scrubbing and part of me was watching myself furiously scrubbing thinking out out damn spots.

And then I realized what an idiot I am what they were and I put one hand on a wet spot and one on my stomach and took a deep breath. Then I took a long shower I stayed in there until the water started turning cold and I stopped crying.

What exactly is a basket case. I mean literally.

When the spots dried they had faded but they were still there. Tomorrow I think I will turn the mattress over that is the best I can do.

Another note for my autobiography autobiographical novel. My senior year in high school we did *The Skin of Our Teeth* for our spring play. I was Mrs. Antrobus although I should have been Sabina and the guy playing Mr. Antrobus and the girl playing Sabina started dating so I thought maybe Henry would like me maybe ask me to the prom but he didn't he went to the prom with Andrea Martin and I ended up going with Matt Crowe uck. I think in my autobiography I will have been Sabina and I will have fallen in love with Mr. Antrobus they get the only kiss of the play.

Skin of our teeth give me some skin it's no skin off my back.

I was in the National Honor Society that is the truth I still have my pin to prove it. What will I say at our five-year reunion are you married no I'm widowed. That shuts just about everybody up they say oh I'm sorry like they killed him then they leave. Do you have any children yes one but I gave it up for adoption. Oh. That will take care of everybody else.

I wonder how many wrinkles on my face I will have by then I don't really have any yet I just have wrinkle-ghosts embryo wrinkles I can tell where they will be when they come. I have horrible wrinkles on my feet the backs of my ankles look like they're fifty sometimes I look at them long and hard then I try to transpose those wrinkles onto my face to see what I will look like. I will have to become a lawyer or something so I can afford plastic surgery. I can't remember if Malone had wrinkles I don't think so but what about his feet I don't know. If he did and they gave the wrinkled skin to a child would the child get wrinkles.

I don't guess I need a will there isn't really anything to will.
What else do you do take care of debts well I will not be
responsible for Malone's debts I've got my own problems.
He bought insurance for himself but they are still trying to
get money out of me well I won't do it that would be like
paying your husband's assassin. I would pay for the funeral
if I live eventually I will $3765 can you believe that our
wedding didn't cost that much but if I die I guess I won't
get around to it.

I would like all my underwear and my makeup to be
thrown away don't give it away. My clothes Mother can

have whatever she wants scarves or belts give the rest to
Goodwill or Salvation Army I don't care which. Same with
the furniture take what you want give the rest away I hope
you take the lamp by our bed I think it would look nice in
your living room. Give my books to Angie she is a good
friend except my Bible Mother might like that and my Hardy
novels give those to Mr. Jackson tell him I thought he might
like them. Give my perfume and my earrings to Camille and
give both of our wedding rings to Malone's mother you can
have them melted down and make something else out of
them or just keep them it's up to you. The rest of my jewelry
especially my opal ring Daddy gave me for high school
graduation also my duck my dishes my kitchen stuff and
everything else there is goes to Mother I think the duck can
be fixed I hope you try to get it fixed. I hope you can get
my book published I hope I will have it totally revised and
typed out by then so you don't have to try to figure out the
order these tapes go in or read over all these horrible erasures
and scratch-out marks I am working on them now as much
as I can. If I am not finished don't do the revisions for me
certain things cannot be revised or the book will be a fake
and only I know what they are. Please give my dictaphone
to the law firm. Maybe you should send it to them as an
anonymous gift put it in a brown wrapper with no return
address. Split all money made on the book equally between
Mother Malone's mother and Daddy's church.

Now I lay me down to sleep I pray the Lord my soul
to keep if I should die before I wake I pray the Lord my
soul to take. God bless Mama and Daddy and Malone and
Malone's mama and Mr. Jackson and Angie and Camille.
And me. And the baby.

If the baby lives get the duck fixed and give her the
duck also my opal ring.

I will write a letter to my mother I will say don't try to raise
the baby give it up for adoption let it have a mother and a

father let it have a chance to be normal. And go on with your own life think about getting married again or traveling you can't grieve forever Daddy wouldn't want you to. Thanks for taking care of me when I was sick. I can't write my mother.

I will write Malone's mother I will say it wasn't like you think I did love him I wouldn't have done anything to hurt him I was just trying to survive. More things had gone wrong than you know about and he wasn't thinking straight it was an accident that neither of us planned neither of us wanted I would do anything to make it not have happened. But it did. It's time to face that and let go please don't hold on to your anger like this. No I can't say that.

Dear God maybe I am coming to You soon maybe when **223** the baby is born. It wasn't suicide I just couldn't make myself go to the doctor I don't know why. Maybe because I know what is coming and I don't want the doctor to confirm it. Maybe because I am afraid the baby is a monster and he would tell me. I don't know. But now I feel that You are preparing me for death so I wanted to talk to You about that.

Please save me. I don't necessarily mean don't make me die I just mean take me to Heaven. And please let Malone and Daddy be there when I get there. I haven't been real religious lately I haven't been to church in a while. But if I had more time I think I would have come to some sort of peace with You. I will do this I am not that scared of dying but would You please help me would You stay with me or send an angel or Malone or somebody to be with me. And would You please take care of the baby don't make the baby die please give it a nice home and parents and let it take piano lessons and be in the school band and grow up and go to college and be happy and get married to somebody nice and have good healthy children and when it dies please let it come to Heaven and be with us. I think she is a girl.

I would name her Elizabeth. When you write her name in the Book of Life could you possibly put Elizabeth in parentheses beside it. If not that's okay.

Don't spend a lot of money on my funeral I will be dead.

*

I can't stand much more of this I just sit around waiting most
of the time even when I am working I'm waiting Angie and
I went to see a movie last night we are starting to become
friends she will probably come to my funeral and the whole
movie I kept thinking I kept trying to figure when it happened when it will come you would think you would know
or at least have some sort of feeling about it but I don't. She
said *how are you feeling* I was very uncomfortable sometimes
when I sit down I need to stand up but when I stand up I
need to sit down and all the time even right after I've gone
to the bathroom I have to go to the bathroom. If Hell is a
personalized thing and the lake of fire is just a metaphor

somebody's Hell will be that they need to go to the bathroom all the time it can drive you crazy. And I said not too good but I went to the doctor's yesterday and he scheduled me for a week from Tuesday and then this will be all over. *That will be good.* Yes. *Will it hurt.* No they do it all with lasers and then they just suck it out I have been telling people this but for some reason when I told Angie I felt gross I felt like saying no I'm lying it's not a tumor it's a baby and I won't let them cut her up I'm her mother but the movie started and the guy in front of us turned around and gave us a look that said shut up or else. When it was over Angie said *do you want to get something to eat* and I said I'm not feeling very good I better go home.

A week from Tuesday I will show up at work and she'll say what happened and I'll say I have an infection so they can't do it until that goes away.

*

I went to Rich's today after work I went in the baby department I looked at all the teeny little clothes I am depressed. I picked up this little pink dress with a mama duck and two baby ducks walking across the front and matching frilled panties and I felt like putting my face in it and screaming but the saleslady came up to me and said *isn't that darling*. And I said yes. And she said *I think it's the cutest thing we have I bought one just like it for my granddaughter*. I smiled. *It would make a beautiful coming-home-from-the-hospital dress*. Do you take checks. *Of course with ID*. So I bought it I don't know why maybe because I kept thinking she was going to ask when are you due and I would say I don't know maybe I just thought buying it would shut her up also I wanted the dress I wanted to take it home and put my face in it and scream. I will give it to the new parents and say please have her picture made in this and send me a copy would they let me do that. I got some makeup on it I will hand-wash it that is better for the baby anyway.

Then I went in the lingerie department and I looked at their prettiest nightgowns the ones for wedding nights that cost $300 and I pretended I was going to buy one no salespeople were there. It was ivory-colored and it looked like it was antique it was almost solid lace and it had a matching robe that tied at the waist with a satin ribbon. This is the kind of thing dentists' wives wear while they're cooking eggs benedict on Sunday morning.

Then I went out into the mall and bought a chocolate chip cookie and a cup of decaffeinated mocha coffee and sat at a table by the fountain. I got the dress out of the bag and made it sit up in the chair beside me and I watched it while I ate my cookie and listened to the music over the loudspeakers. I haven't been very good about not drinking caffeine you shouldn't with a baby but I will be better from now on.

I walked by the bookstore but I decided not to go in and I looked in the pet store but they were out of dogs they only had fish birds and rodents so I left.

Maybe after the baby is born I will take a trip maybe I will drive out to California and get on *Wheel of Fortune* I am Pat Sajak's type and win $35,000 that would help. I watched *Wheel of Fortune* tonight while I was eating dinner the bonus-round phrase was suntan lotion and I knew it before they even started the timer. He could probably help me get my book published. Maybe I will finish my book and then go. I will bring it with me.

Now I think I will pack a suitcase. For the hospital not California. What if Mr. Jackson or somebody finds out and comes to visit me and doesn't call first and I'm wearing one

of my ratty grey nightgowns maybe I should take the dress
back and buy a nightgown not the $300 kind just a pre-
sentable one. Except that I already got makeup on the dress.
Which I could say I noticed when I got home and that's
why I'm taking it back there's an idea. I will have to sleep
on that.

Meanwhile I will plan for a worst-case scenario which
is have a C-section stay in there four to five days then die.

List
1. Seven best panties.
2. Three best nightgowns (or four if buy new one):
   a. Pink polka dots.
   b. Blue granny.
   c. Yellow flowered.
   d. New (optional).
3. Robe.
4. Curlers.
5. Makeup.
6. Deodorant.
7. Bear-claw slippers.
8. UAB T-shirt and sweatpants.
9. Hairbrush.
10. Razor.
11. Three pairs of socks.
12. Baby's dress.
13. Book.
14. Bible.
15. Notebook.
16. Dictaphone and extra tapes.
17. Pink striped dress.
18. Two bras.
19. Slip.
20. Letter to baby.
21. Will.
22. Wendy's phone number.

I will put a note in the pocket of my pink dress please bury me in this if I can fit into it by then. Why do people always bury you in something that is right for that season what do you care after you're dead. My daddy was buried in his light blue summer suit but Malone was buried in his navy blue blazer and grey pants he didn't have a suit but it was a winter outfit. If I wanted to be buried in my favorite sweater black wool with padded shoulders I would have to wait until next winter to die. How do they dress people who already have rigor mortis do they cut the clothes open down the back and sew you back into them they could and no one would ever know because nobody would sit you up and look back there. How long does it take to get rigor mortis do people with arthritis get it faster.

I wonder what I will look like without the baby I can't remember what it was like to have a waist. My breasts have gotten bigger I hope they stay that way certain men like that. I think I will start an exercise program after this.

I don't know what book I will bring maybe *Catch-22* that's a book not just a phrase I have been meaning to read it for a long time maybe some Stephen King.

*

Malone you bastard look what you did to me look what you
did to me before you died and left me to clean up your
mess did you think I was your combination mother and dog.
Because that's how you treated me you jerk. I have been
transcribing my tapes and reading over my notes because I
am going to write an autobiography I will call it a novel but
it is an autobiography and everybody who knows us will
know that and I will expose you for everything you are
everybody will hate you and nobody including me will understand why I took so much shit from you. I will become
famous I will go on *Oprah Winfrey* when she does a show

on abused wives and she will say you were an abused wife what do you advise other abused wives to do. And I will say don't kill your husband and if they try to kill themselves don't let them that is too good for them then you're left to take out the garbage yourself but nobody but nobody should ever put up with what I put up with from Malone and Malone will become a synonym for abusive husband. And then I will say never feel sorry for them they will tell you how tired they are how much they need you how sorry they are. Don't be a fool they don't mean it even when they think they do. Also don't marry what you believe they will become wait until they become it if you want to be married to a dentist for example don't marry a dental student marry a dentist. Do you see what you've done to me Malone do you even feel the least little bit guilty because you should you should be weeping and gnashing your teeth don't ever mention teeth to me again. Before you I wasn't like this I wasn't an angry person I wasn't totally realistic I was a child but you have thrown me into mid-life crisis I am facing my twenty-first birthday and I feel like I have already blown my life.

When you turn twenty-one that is when you should start getting what you wanted out of life you are about to graduate from college and get a good job that pays a lot of money you have a boyfriend and you are thinking about having a huge wedding and getting married you are getting a nice apartment with nice furniture and a nice car you have everything you want. I live in a dump and I am having trouble paying the rent I have a rotten stinking job with no future I have lost my marriage and I am about to lose my baby and here is the worst thing Malone I've lost something I can't even name but it has to do with my capacity to believe in other people and in God. You have robbed me of everything good that was ever in me are you satisfied.

What I want for my birthday:

1. A pearl necklace.
2. A pair of red shoes.
3. A party.
4. A white cake from the bakery with blue roses.
5. To go back to college and this never happened.
6. A teal skirt like Camille's red one and a designer scarf I don't care which designer and I would wear them with my black sweater to my party.

Do you see what you've done Malone are you starting to understand. I want you to know that I know I was a fool but you shouldn't have taken advantage of that you should have protected me. If I had to do it over again wild horses couldn't make me marry you. Which is a strange phrase wild horses couldn't make me do anything but you think of some- **233** thing that could make me do a lot of things and even that couldn't make me marry you again.

I wonder if the baby and I will have the same birthday.

*

I am making progress transcribing my tapes and typing out
my notes in order so I can revise them for the book but I
can hardly do it it's so embarrassing. Maybe I will just leave
Malone out there's hardly a way to rewrite him. Maybe I
will turn Malone into Mr. Jackson and leave Mr. Jackson
out. Of course I will call him Bill that feels funny calling
Mr. Jackson Bill. So I will have to leave out Ann Barton too
and Camille. I think I will leave Angie in she is nicer than
she used to be I don't know why. If I turn Malone into Mr.
Jackson will he be a lawyer or a dental student I don't know
this is becoming extremely complicated. I don't know about
the baby either I am tempted to leave the baby out entirely

but that seems wrong not fair. Plus I can't figure out how to get the background in. Most of the tapes have me talking plus traffic or the dishwasher going or the TV or at least ambulances. Maybe I will have to make this into a play.

I will type for thirty or forty-five minutes every night I typed for an hour and a half tonight and that is too long.

*

I am just killing time. I am waiting anxious for it to come
but also trying to drag it out make it last because when it's
over I will be much lonelier maybe sadder maybe dead. I
have decided not to sell it just give her away give up my
only begotten daughter that she might have life.

I am eating better one banana every day if you eat one
a day and you always eat the worst one it never gets too
bad. It might worry you because you say one morning I will
eat this one and then everything will be perfect but by the
next morning one is getting spotty. But you eat it anyway
you make yourself you don't think about where did those
dots come from what are they exactly when did they get

here you just eat it. So it might worry you but you won't go crazy. Also no more Cokes or coffee until it comes. I think cookies are still okay. I am not going to the doctor because he would just fuss at me for not coming earlier which would cause stress bad for the baby.

I avoid stress on the baby at all cost. I rest whenever I can Mother thinks I'm on my deathbed every time she comes over for the last month now I get in bed so tonight she lets herself in leaves the door open then picks a huge pot of vegetable soup up off the hall floor I'm watching her through the bedroom door and I say hi and she says *I brought you some vegetable soup.* Thank you. *How are you feeling.* A little better. *Well this soup should help would you like a bowl now.* Sure. And she brought it to me on a tray with toast and a glass of milk she can be very nice she loves people when they're sick. She said *did you think about what I asked you last time.* **237** Mother that just wouldn't work please don't take it personally and please don't argue about it right now. *Sweetheart you know I just want what's best for you but I want you to know if you change your mind my door is always open.* Maybe afterwards I will move in with her just for a few days just to make her happy.

This baby better come soon I can't stretch much further.

*

Today is my one-year wedding anniversary.

Today is my twenty-first birthday. Damn.

Someone else's blood is pulsing through my veins.
My blood is pulsing through his veins.
I can't breathe.

*

It is a big mouth a big red mouth stapled shut the staples will fall out it will open up again what will come out this time what have I done what is wrong with me. They cut me open and stapled me shut like I'm paper what is wrong with them.

It is what I did to Malone be sure your sins will find you out I gave him away now I had to give away myself. Termination of rights termination is death I signed my own death warrant I wore a death mask I breathed in the poison I felt myself slipping away I signed my own termination papers why aren't I dead. I felt myself going to Heaven death was tingling happy and life was screaming acute distress acute distress somebody prep her for sleep I was yelling no no no no with nobody listening to me then they lowered the gas mask onto my face and I knew it would kill me so I took long deep breaths as much as I could take I was ready I thought it is finished I lay down my life for my baby I thought I would go to Heaven and be with Daddy and Malone no more sorrow no more pain live in a mansion walk the streets of gold. What happened.

I wish I could start over again I wish I could get married again I wish I could get pregnant again I wish I could make a nursery have a baby shower give out cigars put a blue ribbon on my door I wish it could be born again. I've never been so depressed in my life I'm so depressed I can't move.

They made me take a walk today. First we turned left I am on the end of the hall and we walked past signs for inpatient mental health orthopedics pain management services by which time I was exhausted I said I have to sit down so we sat in a little seating area where there was a rack of brochures one said Outpatient Radiology one said Infertility Problems? You Have Options. I said I want to go back to my room now and somehow we had circled the floor and I had to walk all the way down the maternity floor to get to my room every door has a huge ribbon on it one has two a blue and a pink. Halfway down the hall I started crying so hard they practically had to carry me back to bed.

And the two shall become one flesh. Ye must be born again. I was two now I have become one. Get this two-for-one special the boss says let 'em go. I have to get out of here or I will die this is where Malone died. Malone are you here.

*

Thank-you notes to write:

1. Angie.
2. Malone's mother.
3. The firm.
4. Daddy's church.
5. Malone's church.

I may not write any who cares.

*

I was a roast turkey. Everybody was sitting around me at a banquet table watching TV fixing to take the stuffing out of me but then a warning beep like for bad weather flashed on the TV and then the mouth started screaming acute distress doctor the heartbeat has dropped to sixty-one acute distress and I sat up and looked at the mouth it tried to bite me and everybody at the table jumped up to get a piece of me and I woke up.

It is a boy. He will kill himself. He already tried. He tried to hang himself in my womb he wrapped the umbilical cord around his neck and almost killed himself. Sooner or later he will succeed.

and here are the highlights

I knew this would happen.
I am sleepy as hell.
I go home tomorrow. I will wear my pink striped dress
with the dropped waist.

*

Well here I am again. I can't take all this repetition. I am in a never-ending cycle I have to get out of here. Get out on my own, tragedy hits, go back to Mother, get out on my own, tragedy hits, go back to Mother. And it gets worse every time. Daddy dying was pretty bad but at least it didn't happen to me and then the rape was worse because it did happen to me and then Malone dying was even worse because it didn't happen to me and then the baby was the worst because it did happen to me but I had to sign him over like it didn't happen to me like it never happened at all. But it did and I have the scar to prove it. The baby was worse than the rape because it was total strangers going inside me my own blood overflowing my stomach dripping down to my back replacing it with strangers' blood taking whatever they wanted out of me they knocked me out so they could do whatever they wanted to me and I couldn't fight.

It is over. I will try to write what happened.

I woke up in the middle of the night 1:33 in the morning to be exact I looked at the clock and the bed was wet. Calm down don't think about it. I felt exhausted. I got up. I put some towels on the bed. I changed into a different nightgown. I went back to bed. This time I slept on Malone's side. Except that I couldn't sleep. Every time I closed my eyes I saw millions of teeth. They weren't even in anybody's **247** mouth but they were alive and they were moving around. They were marching around in rows. So I just lay there on Malone's side with my eyes wide open and every time an ambulance went by outside I would follow the lights on the bedroom walls with my eyes until they went away and then I would lie there waiting for another one. There were a lot of ambulances that night.

I slept on and off because I would look at the clock right after I had just looked at it and sometimes no time had passed but sometimes thirty minutes would have passed and that kept happening until 6:30 that morning and then I woke up for good. Except that it didn't feel like I had slept at all. I felt all stiff. I felt like if you ever in your life need a cup of coffee this is one of those times. So I compromised and put a half teaspoon of real and a half teaspoon of decaffeinated in a mug and then I tried to pretend it was all real when I added the water. While it was cooling I put a pop-tart in the toaster and poured a bowl of cereal. Then I turned on the TV and ate breakfast. I am not getting the feel of all this in here. It wasn't just wake up sleepy and make breakfast. It was different. I knew in the back of my mind that something was different. Like I might die today. If it had been a movie there would have been one high shrill note being played constantly in the background.

I called in sick and fifteen minutes later Angie called and asked me if I needed anything. I said no. The rest of the day I didn't talk to anybody. I just lay around on the sofa watching TV feeling strange. I couldn't concentrate. I couldn't even guess the bonus-round phrase on *Wheel of Fortune*. This was only last week. It seems like so long ago that I can't even remember what the bonus-round phrase was. I made a sandwich for lunch and then I felt like I had indigestion so I drank a diet Coke it was caffeine-free. Then I guess I fell asleep on the couch because the next thing I know the baby knees me as hard as it can in the lung. I woke myself up going ugh. It was the hardest it had ever kicked and I was sweating like a madman. So I stood up and I sort of picked up my stomach and tried to move the baby around and it stopped for a while.

Mother had said she would stop by on her way home from work so I thought I better clean up so she wouldn't throw a fit. I made up the bed and took a long cool shower except that halfway through the baby started at it again. It was so bad I was doubled over in the shower. I don't usually make too much noise when I am alone but I couldn't stop saying ow. I said it so much it sounded like I was saying wow wow wow or doing a bad imitation of a dog. I was even practically on all fours.

By the time Mother got there I had pretty much figured out what was going on. Don't ask me why it took me so long. I don't know if I had ever really believed it would happen. Or either I had thought that if it did it would be different more unlike anything else I'd ever felt before. Who would have thought that a person about to come into the world and too much pizza the night before feel like the same thing. So I said Mother don't panic don't ask a lot of questions but please take me to the hospital. Well just as I expected she went berserk. She was absolutely hysterical. I told her I had already packed a suitcase and it was in the bedroom. She picked it up without zipping it closed and everything spilled all over the bedroom floor. I said forget it Mother why don't you come get this later. And she said *no no my daughter is not going to the hospital without her suitcase* and she started packing everything very carefully making sure nothing would be wrinkled. She folded each pair of panties. She folded my bras. She folded my nightgowns one by one. She carefully arranged my curlers and my books in the suitcase. Then she picked up the Rich's bag and dumped the dress out onto the floor. She looked at it like she couldn't figure out what it was. Then she looked at me and she said *baby*. It was horrible. She was crying falling apart. I was crying. I was thinking if we don't go soon the baby's just going to fall out right onto the floor with everything else. And then another one came. The worst one yet. And Mama held my hand and she said *scream if you have to* so I screamed. **249** I screamed a long loud horrible scream. You would think the neighbors would have come over or called the police.

Then I said we have to go. And she threw everything back in the suitcase and zipped it and took me by the arm and we went. I had another one in the car. I started screaming and Mother started pulling over to the side of the road which for one thing you can't do. In that area there is no side of the road except sidewalk plus I thought we may not have that much time and I said through my gritted teeth what are you doing. And she said *I'm pulling over for you.* And I said just get there. So she swerved back into traffic and I thought well maybe we'll have a wreck that will settle everything. But we didn't.

When we got to the hospital Mother dropped me off at the emergency room door and went to find a parking place. It was Malone's emergency room so I started crying again. A man walked up to me and said *do you need some help ma'am.* And I shook my head yes. He said *what's wrong.* I pointed to my stomach and I said the baby's coming. He yelled *Pam* and this woman came over and he said *this woman thinks she's in labor.* I know I'm in labor. Pam said *sit down honey who's your doctor.* I don't know. She gave me a Kleenex and

she said *calm down honey we'll take care of you don't you worry.*
She was rubbing my arm. So I said okay. And she said *now
what's your name.* I told her. *Do you know your doctor's name.* I
looked at my stomach and shook my head no. She said *have
you been to a doctor.* I shook my head no again. *Have you been
to a clinic or anything.* I kept shaking my head. *Have you had
any prenatal care of any kind.* I kept on. *Have you ever been pregnant
before.* I kept shaking. *You've never had a miscarriage.* Shaking.
Do you know how long you've been pregnant. I couldn't talk I just
kept shaking my head. *Do you think you're full-term.* I was trying
to say I don't know but I just shook my head no and tried
to motion I don't know with my hands. I don't know if she
got it. *Can you tell me a little bit about your medical history.* I
shook yes but then Mother comes in and says *are you going
to take care of my baby. Are you her mother. Yes. Look I want you
to go over to admissions and check your daughter in fill out some forms
and things and I will get her examined.* So Mama looked at me
worried but I said I'll be all right and she left.

The next thing I know is they've taken off my clothes
and I'm lying down wearing a sheet in public with this thing
strapped around my stomach and I'm surrounded by people
hunched over me fooling with me all their attention focused
on me but they don't even see me like I'm a frog they are
about to dissect. *Have you had any painkillers has she had any
painkillers.* I kept thinking so this is what you felt like Malone
and I felt sorry for him. I was thinking about him pretending
I was him instead of me as I heard myself screaming all kinds
of horrible things. *Fetal heartbeat. It's been between seventy and
eighty since we started measuring.* Somebody puts an IV in my
hand after three tries and I can see my heartbeat on this
monitor. It is nothing like TV. It is almost flat. And then it
hits me. This is really it. I am dying. My heart isn't beating.
And I feel a little sad a little panic but mostly like that is
just another fact that I will have to live with. *You are dying.
The rent is due. It might thunderstorm tomorrow afternoon.*
Everyone is poking at me.

Then a nurse is saying *doctor the heartbeat has dropped to
sixty-one we have acute fetal distress.* And I thought okay here I

go. And the doctor said *we'll have to do an emergency C-section start prepping her.* Then mass panic. *Prep her for sleep.* I couldn't even watch everybody spinning around. I am rolled on my table into another room the labor and delivery room. They say *can you move over to this table* and I try to get up but I can hardly move I feel like my IV is strapping me to the table or the baby all the sudden weighs two hundred pounds. They are forcing me picking me up practically throwing me onto the other table why can't I just stay on this table. I can see the doctor through a window he is washing his hands he will stick them up me he will stick them inside me grab the baby and pull it out. I feel violated I think of yelling rape. Everybody talking at once. *Relax breathe normally.* I am screaming I might hyperventilate. A man is talking into my ear. *Have you ever had surgery before have you ever been anesthetized I am going to put this nitrous oxide mask over your face I* **251** *want you to breathe normally you will go right to sleep.* It is a death mask. They have shaved me my stomach is cold and wet they are rubbing my stomach with cold wet gauze no one will touch it they won't even touch the gauze. They use metal utensils cooking utensils it is a game to them. I am not a person. I watch the death mask lower onto my face as the doctor walks into the room. I take a deep breath.

The first thing I said when I woke up was oh hell which was the anesthetic talking. You are not responsible for what you say when you have breathed nitrous oxide. A nurse told me later I was saying Malone even while I was unconscious. I was being scrubbed. They were washing my stomach but also my back and I tried not to imagine how or why my back needed washing but I couldn't help it. My stomach was being massaged which hurt like you-know-what. Somebody was talking in my ear saying I have no idea what. My throat felt like when you are about to cry but you are holding it back except that I wasn't about to cry. My stomach felt strange like it wasn't exactly there. I tried to go back to sleep but they wouldn't let me. Some voice said *congratulations you have a six-pound-two-ounce baby boy.* I said swell and it hurt my throat to talk. I never say swell. I don't know if I have ever said swell before that in my life but I said swell. Then my stomach starting hurting like crazy like a dull knife was on the inside sawing to get out and I said oh shit this hurts. And the nurse said *whenever you need painkillers all you have to do is pump it's all connected to a computer that monitors you.* So I pumped and pumped I thought I might kill myself. And she said *that's all it will give you right now you're still under anesthetic.* And I thought you liar you said I could have all I wanted but I didn't say anything because it hurt my throat plus I was too tired.

I guess I slept the rest of the night. A nurse told me later that I pumped for painkillers even when I was asleep. My throat hurt because they had put a tube down it. What else did they do. I can't think about it.

The next day actually later that same day because it was the next day by then anyway later this cheery nurse came in and said *breakfast in bed* practically singing and that $300 nightgown flashed in my head and I looked at her trying to say shut up without words. And she said *it's just ice chips but it will feel good on your throat.* I said is my baby alive. The nurse said *of course and he's just beautiful section babies usually are prettier because they never have forceps bruises where some vaginal deliveries get elongated misshapen heads when they go through the birth canal.* I thought this is more than I wanted to know. Then she said *did they tell you about him.* Not looking at her not even thinking anything just seeing images of a baby with one arm or one leg or a lopsided face. And she started helping me get up making me get up and said *no no no it's nothing that unusual but I just wanted to tell you before you saw him that he is in isolation in intensive care because the doctor wants to watch him for infection so you'll have to scrub before you hold him.* Why is he in intensive care. *Just because the doctor wants to watch him now just so you'll know what to expect his face is going to have a little blue tint and some little blue dots but that's going to fade real soon and he is connected to monitors so he's got some wires taped to him so don't let it upset you it's not as bad as it looks.* What's wrong with him. *I don't think anything is wrong really except that he is a little depressed which is normal in this kind of situation see when mama gets gas baby gets gas and he'll have to sleep it off just like you.* How can he be depressed when he is one day old and I started crying because I saw the future. She explained some garbage about anesthesia but I had heard all I wanted to hear. I said just take me to him.

They put my baby in an oven. They taped wires to him and didn't give him any clothes and they put him in an oven almost a coffin and made him squirm around like a wet rat. It was the most degrading thing I had ever seen. You are born and you die in humiliation. I started crying again and she took me back to my room and I said I need to be alone. They had teeny little wires attached to his chest and his stomach and his foot. They put a straw in your foot Malone and your soul fell out. I couldn't tell who he looked like. He didn't look like either of us he didn't even look **253** human.

About a half hour later I called Wendy. I think I'm ready to give my baby up for adoption. *Why don't I come meet you and we'll talk about it.* Come to UAB hospital room 614. Then I sat there in my bed waiting for her for fifteen minutes. I felt like I was waiting for a firing squad. Mother called. She had stayed up all night. I said Mother get some rest I'll sleep all morning and I'll probably need you this afternoon.

Wendy was there within fifteen minutes. She walked in the room and said *hi I'm Wendy* and came over to shake my hand and touched my arm instead when she saw my IV. I don't think she knew that I was the novelist. She said *how ya doing.* I said okay. She was fatter and plainer looking than I expected and somehow her accent seemed thicker in person than over the phone. I said where did you grow up. *Pineapple.* Pineapple. *Pineapple Alabama.* I never heard of that. *Most people haven't it's a teeny little town.* Where is it. *The closest thing most people know is Greenville because everybody from Birmingham stops for lunch in Greenville on their way to Florida.* Yeah we used to stop there every summer and get turkey sandwiches. *Well Pine-*

apple's not too far from there. Oh. Silence. *Where were you raised.*
I lived in Birmingham all my life except when I went away
to college for a while. *I've just lived here for a year since I graduated
from college but it's a nice place once you get used to all these huge
buildings.* Where'd you go to college. *Auburn.* Did you like it.
I loved it. I want to go to Georgia. *University of Georgia.* Yeah.
Oh you'll love it. Yeah. Silence. She walked over to the window. *You have a nice view of the parking lot here.* I hadn't noticed.
At least it's interesting you can watch people. Yeah. Silence. She
sat down in the hospital chair. *Want to talk about it.* I don't
know. She put her hand on the bed. She wore a ring with
two pearls. *I know what you're going through is real hard and I
want you to know that I'm here to help you whatever you need.* I had
liked her but she started reminding me of Carolyn. I got
this image of her driving a ten-year-old yellow Camaro with
a bumper sticker that said God is Awesome and I tried to
put it out of my mind. I just think I ought to give up the
baby. *Well can you tell me a little bit about your situation.* I looked
at her. *Like does the father agree with your decision.* My husband.
He died. *Oh I'm sorry bless your heart what happened.* It was an
accident he died right here. *And you think it would be best for
the baby to have two parents.* I shook my head yes. She started
rubbing my arm. *This is a very loving unselfish act you are doing.*
I shook my head yes. *You know I believe in God and I believe that
He has a plan for each one of us and I believe that He won't let you
suffer like this unless it's for a reason I mean I believe that He will use
this suffering now to bless you later I really do.* I was still shaking
my head yes. *What you're doing is a good thing you should feel
really proud.* I put my face in my hands. I shook my head no.
She was rubbing my back. I pumped the computer and she
handed me a Kleenex. I blew my nose. Silence. He's a little
boy who needs good parents who won't get divorced who
will take good care of him who will give him clothes and
play baseball with him and never let him get depressed I
know him and I know that he has a tendency to get depressed
and they have to be people who know how to deal with
that. I think he needs me I can't do this. And I tried to slump
under the covers but it hurt my stomach to move so I pulled

them up as far as I could over my face. She kept rubbing my back. I pumped the computer again. *It's a big confusing decision.* My face was in the covers in my hands. I shook yes and wiped my nose with the sheet. She gave me another Kleenex. Silence. She said *would you like me to tell you how adoptions work.* I shook yes. *Well first of all there are millions and millions of people who would love to adopt right now the waiting lists are unbelievable and we go through them and screen them very carefully we only take the very best parents. Before we try to match a couple with a baby we have interviewed them five or six times we have made sure that at least one of them has a stable job but that they have enough time for the baby and we have had them examined by a psychologist to determine their mental and emotional stability so that when we put a baby with parents we know and you can know that he's going to a good loving home. And then we don't just leave you in the lurch. We will provide a family for you to live with for a while if you need that* **255** *to get back on your feet and we provide individual and group counseling where you can meet other girls who have gone through what you are going through.* I kept thinking of that Saturday with Kenny and Carolyn and I said no. *You don't want to do that.* No. *Well of course it's up to you but we will do everything for you that we can to make your transition back into normal life as painless as possible.* Silence. She was still rubbing. *You also have the option of corresponding anonymously with the parents because we recognize that what you are doing is giving up a part of yourself and you'll probably want some news about how the baby is doing every so often.* I can't. *I'll be honest with you I'm not going to tell you it's not hard because it might be the hardest thing you ever do but I will tell you that it might be the most loving most unselfish thing you ever do.*

It might be. Or it might be the most hateful most selfish thing I ever did. What kind of anonymous correspondence would we have. *Dear Donor, Thank you for the very special gift you have given our family. We will always be grateful to God for the gift of life you have given us. We imagine that you are experiencing a great personal loss at this time, and we hope that knowing how much joy your tragedy has brought to others will be some sort of consolation to you. Please know that you are in our prayers blah blah blah.* Give me a break.

You have to sign some papers and terminate your rights. You terminate your right to love him your right to hold him your right to be what you already are his mother. It's not so simple to terminate the rest of you.

Mother was devastated. She needs to go for counseling. She is not my problem. Why did I do it. What is wrong with me. I can't give birth right. I can't be a mother right. I can't do anything right. This is pitiful.

You can write down on paper that you are not your son's mother but that doesn't make it true.

*

I have been trying to think of titles they won't tell me what his name is. I have been trying to concentrate on my book I need to get it finished it has to have a title and an ending and then I will be done I work on it all the time now. I want something that encompasses everything the whole life cycle from conception to death the inheritances we thought we were getting from Daddy and Malone's granddaddy and my duck and the baby's legacy of suicide what it will inherit even though it's not really in this family anymore and everything that keeps being passed on from generation to generation all the chains that bind us even when we're not aware.

The Chains That Bind. No. What about *Heredity* which isn't quite right it doesn't have a ring to it.

       What Is Close to Heredity in the Dictionary
hereafter
hereby
hereditary
heredity
herein
hereof
heresy
heretic
heretofore
hereupon
herewith
heritable
heritage
hermaphrodite
Nothing that works for a title. I wonder what they call him. While I'm typing my notes and transcribing my tapes I keep on the lookout for a good phrase. So far nothing. Maybe I'm not cut out to be a writer after all.

    My tape fell off today. When they took out my staples they replaced them with tape. Am I coming unglued.

    Maybe I will cut the baby from the manuscript. You can't bring in a new character that late in a novel. Maybe I will make it go from our wedding day to Malone's death I will call it Death of a Marriage.
              Death of a Marriage
No forget it.

*

Mother made me go to the doctor today. It was horrible. My second husband may be a lawyer but he will definitely not be a doctor. He says I am healing remarkably I can drive starting next week and go back to work the week after that. Which gave me a stomachache.

After the doctor Mother took me to the mall for lunch and we went to Rich's. She returned the baby dress and I stayed in ladies' clothes. We bought me a fall sweater with the money and she paid the difference. It's real pretty. It makes me sad.

✳

Wendy stopped by today. That's her phrase. She said *how you getting along*. Well Wendy I thought what can I say for two weeks now I have been lying around with someone else's blood pumping through me I can't eat what I want I can't drive I still can't walk normally sometimes I feel dizzy and I wonder if my head is getting enough of his or her blood or is only my blood going to my head and there isn't enough to go around maybe mine and theirs don't get along together maybe they were in such a hurry that they put in the wrong blood type and I will drop dead any second now maybe I have AIDS do you know what this is like Wendy do you know what it's like to wonder next time you bleed will you recognize it or will it be darker my blood has always been exceptionally bright. I said fine. She said *can I do anything for you* only she said ya. Well Wendy I thought what could you do could you make this not have happened do you have that power can you rewrite history because if you can't there's not a damn thing you can do. The fact is that he was a real live baby boy my own flesh-and-blood son inside me and now he's gone forever three generations gone forever my father my husband my son but this is the worst one the others I can say God did it I had no way of controlling the situation but this one I signed him away myself and now I have a built-in permanent scar to remind me every time I take a shower as if I might forget and there is nothing that anybody can do I just have to live with it. I said I guess not. She stayed anyway and talked for about forty-five minutes then she went and talked to Mother for I don't know **261** how long I fell asleep. She said she'll stop by again next week. Swell.

It seems sort of primitive like I participated unknowingly and unwillingly I might add in some ancient ritual and now some other tribe is raising my child and the blood of their tribe is running through my veins. I have got to stop thinking about this I try very hard not to think about this. I wonder if it could be Malone's blood. I wonder how he is doing if he knows about his son if he has disintegrated yet.

I wonder if I will get to choose the type style and the ink color for the book. Of course I know it will be black but I'm talking about the shade there are many shades of black. I would like something not so light that it strains your eyes but as light as possible I don't like heavy letters on a page where if you squint the letters run together and the page turns black. You know the phrase bleeding ink I keep thinking of that for a title I know it's an awful title but also I'm afraid if I used it I would get some joker for a printer and he would use a dark dark black so the ink would bleed.

I'm done. I now have an entire manuscript ready to be revised. Here is what I will do:
1. Change names:
   Mark to Malone
   Marian to Camille
   Ginny to Angie
   Mr. Robertson to Mr. Jackson
   Raymond to Rusty
   Chuck to Claire
   Christine Dominick to Ann Barton
   Mr. Waters to Mr. Brooks

Mr. Baldwin to Mr. Ballard

me to?

Raymond and Chuck will hate that.

2. Start with wedding. Make it huge. Seven bridesmaids. Five-foot train on my gown. A band with dancing. Honeymoon on Bahamas.

3. Mark will already be a dentist and I will be a lawyer. We own a four-bedroom house in Mountain Brook with a swimming pool and we give parties full of dentists and lawyers all the time.

4. Maybe Mark should be a lawyer and I'm a housewife and we have a baby which would make it sadder when he dies.

5. Mr. Robertson is Mark's best friend so he is over at our house all the time.

6. Raymond and Chuck never existed.

7. His father died of a heart attack.

8. My father was a business tycoon and left me a trust fund. My mother lives in a better house. Not Mountain Brook but maybe Homewood or Vestavia.

9. Add ending.

I have a lot of work to do. I will do the names first. First thing tomorrow. I will finish before I go back to work.

epilogue

If you have been reading this book and you are not my mother I guess that means it got published. I am glad. This morning I got out of bed and changed all the names which believe it or not took me all day. Then I reread Chapter One and I said how in the world am I ever going to turn this into a book before I have to go back to work how am I going to take out what I want to take out and have it still make sense how am I going to end it I can't even think of an ending and I got so depressed that I turned on the TV and I watched *Star Search* and ate a bowl of cereal. I spilled some milk on my notes but I didn't care although I did wipe it up and I said to myself it's over. Face facts. This chapter of your life has ended so let it. And I realized that it would take me as long to revise this manuscript as it did to write it which is almost a year and life is too short. So I turned to the last page of my transcription and I read over the list of things I've left undone and one by one I forgave myself for them. And then I wrote a real fancy The End because ultimately that is all you can do you can kill yourself trying to come up with the perfect ending and then it turns out fake or you can say that's all there is so it's the end and make the best of it. Think about beginnings not endings nothing ever ends. From now on I move forward not back.

So I will get dressed drive down to the library xerox the first page of agents' addresses from *The Writer's Market* go home pick the best-looking one off the page and send it to her I will pick a woman. I will write Requested MS all over the envelope and my cover letter will say Dear Agent X, Enclosed please find the only existent copy of my book manuscript. Please read it and sell it to a publisher. I would like for it to be published under another name because it is my past and I am ready to move into my future, and I would like for it to make about $200,000. Also I can't think of a title. Anything you want to call me and it is fine with me. I'm sure you understand. Good luck.

You have to give the Catholics credit for one thing they have saints for everything very convenient. When I put it in the parcel slot at the post office I will pray that God will let the agent like it. If only I could ask the saint of manuscripts the saint of books the saint of agents to help I would feel better so just in case I will say Saint What's-Your-Name go with this. I bet Bartholomew is the saint of people who have been skinned I bet he and Mark are big buddies.

. . .

If I ever write another book I will tell you what became of me and if the baby has contacted me by then I will tell you what became of him. Right now I am just contemplating my options. I will buy a new notebook on the way home from the post office and list them on the first page.

Bookmark

The text of this book was set in the typeface Weiss and the display was set in Franklin Gothic Extra Condensed by Crane Typesetting Service, Inc., West Barnstable, Massachusetts.

It was printed on 55 lb Glatfelter, an acid-free paper, and bound by Berryville Graphics, Berryville, Virginia.

DESIGNED BY CHIP KIDD